Cleopa~
Escape Dow~

CAROLINE CORBY was born and brought up in London. She studied mathematics and statistics at Bristol University, then became a banker and spent thirteen years in the City, ending up as a director in a venture capital company before deciding to leave her job to spend more time with her young family.

Caroline has always enjoyed history and wanted to find a historical novel aimed at children that would capture her daughter's imagination. After searching without success, she decided to write one herself and the Before They Were Famous series was born. It explores the early lives of some of history's most fascinating characters, who, in shifting, dangerous worlds, struggle to make their mark and become heroes of the future. Of *Cleopatra: Escape Down the Nile*, Caroline says: "I knew Cleopatra led an extraordinary life but the more I researched her, the more intrigued I became by this brave and clever young queen."

Caroline lives in Hampstead, North London, with her husband and three daughters aged fourteen, twelve and ten.

Other titles in the series

CAROLINE CORBY

CLEOPATRA

Escape Down the Nile

WALKER
BOOKS

First published 2008 by Walker Books Ltd
87 Vauxhall Walk, London SE11 5HJ

2 4 6 8 10 9 7 5 3 1

Text © 2008 Caroline Corby
Cover design © 2008 Walker Books Ltd
Girl photo: Glow Images/Alamy

This book has been typeset in Usherwood and Herculanum

Printed by Cox and Wyman Ltd, Reading, Berkshire

British Library Cataloguing in Publication Data:
a catalogue record for this book is available from the British Library

ISBN: 978-1-4063-1033-7

www.walkerbooks.co.uk

For Scout

59BC

THE GIRL lay still. Something had woken her, she wasn't sure what. Moonlight peeped through the cracks in her shutters. In the silvery light everything seemed as usual. She could hear the familiar snores of her nursemaid next door – but that wasn't it. Iras snored every night. The girl rolled onto her side to try and settle, and as she did so she heard an angry "hiss". She froze – there it was again. And now through her linen sheet she felt a weight, like a heavy rope, slide over her ankle. Her heart pounded. She lifted her head as slowly as she could. At the foot of her bed was a long snake with a body as thick as her arm.

Like every child in Egypt, Cleopatra had been warned about snakes. In the cold winter months they slipped into houses looking for warm places to hide. Most weren't dangerous but a few could kill with a single bite. And now there was one only inches away from her. Her instinct was to scream for help, but her guard was outside the door and Iras was in the next room. If it were poisonous neither would be fast enough to save her.

Calm down, she told herself, *it's probably just a grass snake*. But what if it wasn't? She needed to know its colour. Green was harmless. Black meant trouble. But it was impossible to be sure in the moonlight.

Her back was beginning to ache from holding the same position but she dared not move. Suddenly there was a loud knock.

"Princess! Princess!"

It was Apollodorus, her guard. What was he doing pounding on her door in the middle of the night?

The snake reared up, agitated by the noise. It was hissing frantically and she could feel its body swaying against her leg. Cleopatra prayed her guard would go away, but instead he opened the door, letting in a shaft of light from a burning torch.

"Princess, are you awake?"

The snake rose higher and suddenly flared its head into a flat hood. There was no doubt any more. Cleopatra knew exactly what it was – a deadly cobra, angry enough to strike.

CLEOPATRA braced herself for the prick of the cobra's fangs, but instead she felt the heat of a burning torch skimming past her head. It landed on the snake's coils and the creature retreated, flicking its tail. Cleopatra took her chance and leapt away. In the same moment, Apollodorus drew his sword and expertly decapitated the animal.

"Princess Cleopatra, are you all right?" he asked as he pushed the headless snake away from her with the point of his blade.

Before she could answer, a dark-skinned, plump woman dressed only in a nightgown came in and shrieked.

"Cleopatra's bed's on fire! Apollodorus, do something!"

The tall, fair man took off his cloak and smothered the remaining embers from the torch. The room filled with the acrid smell of singed wool.

"What's going on?" asked Iras, horrified.

Cleopatra and Apollodorus explained as best they could.

"Come here," said Iras, holding out her arms. "To think you could have been killed tonight."

"I'm fine – thanks to Apollodorus. Honestly," said

Cleopatra. Her heart was still racing but the drama was over.

"But you're shaking," protested her nurse.

"It's the cold night air," said Cleopatra, who didn't want Iras to fuss. "That's why the snake came in – to get warm."

"I suppose so," said Iras, "but I've never heard of a cobra coming into a house in the city. It's the kind of thing that used to happen in the village where I grew up, not in a place like Alexandria."

"And we're three floors up," added Apollodorus grimly.

"What are you saying?" asked Cleopatra, dreading the answer.

"What I'm saying," said her guard, "is that someone must have put that cobra in your room deliberately."

"THANK goodness you heard Cleopatra shouting," said Iras to Apollodorus as she cleared up the remains of the burnt sheet.

"I didn't. She didn't make a sound."

"That's right," said Cleopatra. She remembered she'd been far too frightened of disturbing the snake to call out. "So why did you come in? It must be very late."

"With all this drama I forgot to tell you. I have a message from the king. Your stepmother is dying. You're to go to her rooms at once."

"How can Queen Selene be dying?" Cleopatra was bewildered. "I saw her last week and she looked fine."

"I don't know," said Apollodorus. "But those are my instructions."

"Are you sure that the king wants her?" asked Iras. "She's very young to witness a departure into the next life."

"I'm eleven," said Cleopatra. "That's old enough, and I have to go if Father has summoned me."

"True," said Iras with a weary sigh. She passed Cleopatra a bowl and flannel.

"Wash that soot off while I get you some clothes. Apollodorus, please leave us."

Cleopatra wiped her cheeks and forehead with the cloth distractedly.

The queen is dying, she thought over and over again. It didn't seem possible. For six years Queen Selena had been the rock Cleopatra's father leant on. She had encouraged him to concentrate on the business of ruling rather than pleasure, had given him three more children and had even managed to curb his drinking. Although she had not shown much interest in Cleopatra or the other children of the king's first wife, she had never deliberately set out to harm them either. Another stepmother could have been a lot worse. Life at court would be very different without her.

The wooden door creaked on its hinges and Iras reappeared carrying a bundle of clothes. Cleopatra quickly finished washing.

"Put these on."

Iras had chosen a simple white toga with a gold brooch which clipped neatly over the folds of the dress. Cleopatra put it on and sat down on a stool in front of a large, polished mirror.

"Look at the state you're in. You reek of smoke. There's no time for a bath but let me at least untangle you."

Iras began brushing her unruly, brown hair. Usually Cleopatra would protest that she could do it herself, but not tonight. She hardly noticed the tugs. She was too preoccupied.

"Iras, Father needs the queen. What will he do without her?"

"I hope he doesn't go back to the drink. That's the last thing we need," Iras answered, plaiting two small bunches. She wound them around Cleopatra's head, her hands working efficiently.

"If she does die, do you think he'll choose a new wife?"

"How should I know?" said her nurse, sounding tired.

Cleopatra sighed. It was so hard to find out what was happening at court. It was only by eavesdropping or badgering Iras that she learnt anything. She tried to keep an ear open, particularly when the servants didn't know she was listening. This way she'd discovered that her father was desperately short of money; she'd heard two soldiers moaning that they hadn't been paid all year. And he was not popular. Why else had some slaves cleaning her floor laughed about "that mighty king who doesn't dare leave his own palace"? But these were only random snippets. She might not hear of any marriage plans for weeks.

There was a loud knock.

"Who is it?" called Iras.

Apollodorus appeared at the door.

"The princess's escort is here."

"They must wait a minute. I'm not quite finished."

The door was unceremoniously pushed open and a tall man with a crooked nose entered. He was dressed in the uniform of the Egyptian army and had a dagger at his waist.

"You've had plenty of time," he barked.

It was General Achillas. Looking as if she might faint, Iras fell to her knees.

"I'm sorry, Sir. I had no idea that you were outside or I would never have spoken in that way," she said, all in a rush.

"I dare say you wouldn't," he answered coldly.

He looked around the room, his eyes moving from the burnt bed to the blood spots left by the cobra on the polished floor. Cleopatra could see a vein throbbing in his thick neck as he surveyed the scene, but he asked no questions.

There was an awkward silence.

This night is so strange, thought Cleopatra. First that snake, and then the news of Queen Selene, and now General Achillas, one of the most powerful men in Egypt, in her room.

Achillas turned.

"Let's go," he said grimly, pointing them towards the door.

GENERAL Achillas led the way in silence through the labyrinthine palace. He kept up such a fast pace that Cleopatra had to jog beside him. Her stomach tightened with nerves – she had never witnessed a death before.

They were getting close to the queen's quarters. Cleopatra looked curiously at the ornate walls for it was a part of the palace that she rarely visited. And then, without warning, General Achillas turned left.

"Aren't the queen's rooms the other way?" she asked.

"I think I know my way around," Achillas answered tetchily. "I'm collecting Princess Berenike."

Cleopatra groaned inwardly. Berenike was always so patronizing and rude. She was only six years older than Cleopatra but she acted as if her sister were a different species. If only they had to collect Tryphaena instead. As the eldest of the king's children, Tryphaena's time was much in demand but whenever she saw Cleopatra she was always considerate and patient. Cleopatra secretly thought of her as the mother she'd never had.

They soon reached a cedar door decorated with heavy, gold bolts. It was opened by a young woman of extraordinary beauty. Her glossy, black hair was ornately arranged and her turquoise toga perfectly matched the crystal blue of her cold eyes. Berenike didn't bother with a greeting. She seemed annoyed to see her younger sister.

"What's she doing here?" she asked Achillas.

"The king told me to bring you both. I hope you don't mind."

Cleopatra couldn't help noticing the contrast between the way Achillas had spoken to her and the respectful tone he used to her sister.

"You'd better come in," snapped Berenike.

She turned to Cleopatra.

"I have some business with the general. Wait here."

The door was firmly closed leaving her with Iras and two soldiers in the flame-lit corridor. They could hear Berenike's raised voice.

"She's giving him hell," said Iras softly, slipping naturally from Greek, the language spoken at court, into her native Egyptian.

Cleopatra nodded, but she had something else on her mind.

"Iras, don't you think it's strange that Achillas didn't ask what had happened in my room tonight?"

"He's a soldier. He's seen it all before," said Iras.

"But he didn't say anything," said Cleopatra. "It's almost as if he were expecting it."

The thought was disturbing. "You don't think he could have had anything to do with the snake, do you?"

Iras quickly flashed her eyes to the soldiers and back

as if to say, "Don't say any more in front of them."

This exasperated Cleopatra; *Iras knows the guards won't understand*, she thought. *Why is she being so silly?* Few people at court spoke anything other than Greek and, despite her family ruling Egypt for three hundred years since conquering the country, Cleopatra was the first Ptolemy to speak the native language. This she owed to her mother, who had appointed Iras, a local woman, as nursemaid to her third baby. It had become second nature to Cleopatra to slip from Greek to Egyptian when she was saying something to her nurse she didn't want anyone else to hear.

Just then the door swung open and Berenike appeared with a leopard cub in her arms. Its spotted fur was still fluffy; it couldn't have been more than a few weeks old.

"You've got a new pet," said Cleopatra, reaching out to stroke the cub's head.

It growled and nipped her finger before she could pull it away. Its teeth were like razors.

Berenike chuckled and patted the animal.

"Good girl."

She fed it a cube of raw meat.

"That thing's dangerous," said Cleopatra. "You should send it to the trainer."

"No, I'm doing it myself. Nefer will only let one person touch her and that's me."

Berenike tied a gold chain to the leopard's collar.

"Stay here, my beauty. I can't take you to a deathbed, I don't trust you not to nip the corpse." She laughed. "Iras, you are dismissed. Come now, Cleopatra, let's go. We can't keep the king waiting any longer."

A FEW oil lamps had been lit but much of the room was in shadow. Against the far wall was a bed with white cotton hangings round it. A pitiful moan came from behind the curtains. Cleopatra knew that it must be the queen and she dreaded seeing her.

The room was crowded with courtiers. In the centre stood her father, King Ptolemy the Twelfth, wearing the gold serpent crown and a toga of royal purple. His hair was in tight black curls with just a hint of grey and his face was clean shaven. Cleopatra was sad to see that there was a glass of wine in his hand – with the king it was always wine and she hated the way it changed him. When he was sober he was kind and relaxed and she enjoyed her visits to his rooms, but when he was drunk it was another story. He could be cruel or outrageous or, worse still, so vague it was as if he didn't know she was there.

The princesses dropped to their knees and kissed the floor in front of the king's feet.

"So you're here at last." He swayed as he spoke. "What took you so long?"

Her father was in a temper. Cleopatra could see a nerve in his cheek twitching with irritation.

"I'm afraid that Cleopatra's maid took forever getting her ready," Berenike answered, before anyone else could say a word.

Cleopatra felt a sharp pinch on the back of her thigh. It was so like Berenike. She always avoided getting into trouble; like the time she'd knocked over a candle and destroyed the king's favourite tapestry. Cleopatra had seen her do it and yet somehow Berenike had contrived for her to get the blame. The pinch was a warning: don't you dare say a word. But Cleopatra was not going to put up with it tonight.

"Father, I was ready—"

"Sister," interrupted Berenike, "I'm sure the king does not want to be bothered with such trivial matters now."

"Quite right. Next time I summon you, be here straight away. Now get up."

How did Berenike always manage to look so innocent in front of their father? It was so unfair, but Cleopatra bit her tongue. This was not the time to be squabbling.

"Now where's Tryphaena?" asked Ptolemy. "Can't anybody be bothered to come when I send for them?"

"She must have overslept. I'll send a soldier to hurry her up," said Berenike soothingly. "Would you like Arsinoe and the little princes as well?"

"No, of course not. They're far too young," said the king.

He didn't need to add that while Cleopatra and Berenike were witnessing the death of a queen, for the little ones it would be the death of their mother.

Just then a scream pierced the room. The king winced.

"Come," he said. "It is time for the ceremony to begin."

Cleopatra followed her father over to the carved, ebony bed and watched him pull aside the curtains.

The queen lay, clutching her stomach, sometimes moaning softly and sometimes crying out. Her body was twisted and emaciated. Cleopatra could hardly believe the transformation that had taken place since she had last seen her. Then she had been a powerful consort who made men tremble in her presence. Now she was pitifully frail.

Bald-headed priests in flowing, white robes began chanting and the moans and chants wove together until they filled the room with their unhappy tune. Cleopatra felt like crying. Seven years before, a similar ceremony must have been held for her mother in the very same room – Tryphaena and Berenike had been present but she had been too small. Now she was grateful. She would hate to have more memories like these.

An odd rasping sound brought her attention back to the bed. Queen Selene was gasping for breath. Cleopatra began counting these unnerving gulps of air, to calm the tension rising in her.

"One, two, three..." she counted, "...six, seven..."

She paused, waiting for the next one, but it never came.

6

"TAKE the queen to the House of Beauty," commanded the king.

He sounded worn out. They were all exhausted.

Cleopatra watched as the high priest, Pshereni, instructed his men to remove the queen to the temple where over the next two months her body would be embalmed. She couldn't help feeling repelled whenever she saw this man. She knew that she shouldn't, after all he was the most senior priest in Egypt, but he made her flesh creep. Perhaps it was the heavy, black kohl around his eyes, or his leopard skin tunic, or maybe it was knowing that he spent so long with corpses. She could just imagine him forcing a hook through someone's nose and draining the brain away or pulling out organs from a limp stomach. Iras always tutted if Cleopatra said such things to her. "He doesn't do it himself, he only oversees it," she'd tell her, but it didn't change Cleopatra's mind.

The first signs of daybreak were now visible through the shutters. King Ptolemy ordered them to be opened and the dimness gave way to the grey light of dawn. Just then there was a commotion at the door. Tryphaena was in such a hurry that she'd almost knocked the queen's body off its stretcher.

She arrived in a dressing gown with her hair unbrushed.

"Father, I'm so sorry I wasn't here in time! I wasn't told."

The king picked up a jug and refilled his goblet.

"Really?" he said coldly. "I asked Achillas to fetch you and then Berenike sent a soldier when you didn't appear."

"Nobody knocked on my door, Father, I swear," said the princess.

"Perhaps they couldn't rouse you from your sleep," said Berenike.

Tryphaena flashed her sister an angry glance.

"I'm sure I would have heard. Father, please forgive me."

The king nodded curtly.

"It's a sad day. Once Arsinoe and the little princes are up, I will break the news to them myself. Now go back to your rooms and try to get some rest." He turned to Tryphaena and added sarcastically, "Those of you that need it."

Cleopatra saw Tryphaena blush and a faint smile pass across Berenike's face. Berenike had made sure that Tryphaena wasn't there on time. What Cleopatra didn't know was how or why.

7

TRYPHAENA accompanied Cleopatra back to her rooms. As soon as they were inside the apartment she threw open the shutters. The window looked directly over the sea.

"The lighthouse looks so huge from here. Come and look."

Above them gulls squawked noisily in the dawn light.

"Nobody can hear us, can they?" Tryphaena whispered urgently. "Not even your guard outside?"

The wind whipped around them, blowing the curtains horizontal and sending a pile of papyrus flapping across the marble floor. Cleopatra could hardly hear herself.

"No, of course not," she said. "What is it?"

Why was her sister behaving so oddly? Normally she was gentle and calm. After their mother died, the king had relied on Tryphaena to take care of the younger ones because she was the sensible, dependable daughter. But now she seemed strained and anxious.

"I'm being followed by Berenike's spies. Even some of my own guards are working for her."

"Are you sure?"

"Yes. It's been going on for weeks now," said Tryphaena sadly. "And you saw the way she was tonight. Has anything peculiar happened to you?"

Cleopatra thought of the cobra and Achillas's strange reaction. She told her sister what had happened.

"You think he put the snake there?" asked Tryphaena.

"I don't know," said Cleopatra. "I just have a feeling, that's all. It certainly didn't get there by itself."

Tryphaena nodded thoughtfully.

"If Achillas is involved then it's on Berenike's orders. Those two are as thick as thieves."

"But why?"

"She's desperate to rule Egypt. Her plan is to step into Queen Selene's shoes."

"Marry Father?" Cleopatra looked shocked. "If he were to choose to marry a relative again, it would be you, surely. You're the eldest daughter."

Along with their religion, Cleopatra's ancestors had adopted the Pharaoh's practice of marrying within the family. Kings married mothers, siblings or daughters. Cleopatra's own mother and father had been brother and sister.

"I don't care whether I'm chosen," said Tryphaena. "I don't want to be queen, it's just that I know how awful Berenike would be."

Cleopatra believed her – Tryphaena was too kind to be ambitious.

"Cleopatra, from now on you must be especially

vigilant. The queen's sudden illness is suspicious and now there's the snake and me being spied on. Maybe it's worse than I thought. Maybe she's planning to get rid of all of us so she has no rivals."

"You really think she would?" Cleopatra said.

She knew Berenike could be brutal and that she was unreasonable and beat her servants over the slightest mistake. One young girl had been covered in bruises just for overheating a bath; another had been whipped for dropping a plate. But this was something else entirely.

Tryphaena looked sadder than ever.

"Yes, I'm sorry but I do."

"Then we must go to Father," said Cleopatra. "Surely he'll stop it."

"He won't believe it. We need proof."

"How can we get it?" asked Cleopatra, dismayed.

"I don't know yet, but until we do, we must stay away from each other. My guards report my every movement and we mustn't make Berenike suspicious."

Cleopatra was worried. How could she protect herself from a second visit from a snake?

Tryphaena saw the doubt in her eyes. She took her hands.

"Is there anybody you can trust?"

"Yes. Iras and Apollodorus. They'd never betray me." There was no doubt in Cleopatra's mind.

"Then tell them of this conversation. Now I must go

but, remember, whatever lies ahead we must remain loyal to Father. He's not perfect but he is the king."

"Of course I'll stay loyal. He's our father."

"Good," said Tryphaena, and Cleopatra was surprised to see her eyes fill with tears. She couldn't bear it. It was as if her sister was saying a final goodbye.

"Tryphaena, you'll be careful too, won't you?" she said earnestly.

Tryphaena took her in her arms and hugged her briefly.

"Of course I will. Try not to worry. I'll get a message to you when I can but until then you must be patient."

8

IT was early morning when Cleopatra climbed into the litter to go to the Museion, the city's famous university, where she was a student. Apollodorus took her hand to help her into her seat.

"Thank you," she said, settling onto a cushion.

Now that she had told Iras and Apollodorus of Tryphaena's worries, she was rarely out of their sight. Although it was comforting, it was also frustrating. She never had a moment to herself.

A week had passed and Cleopatra had still not heard from Tryphaena. But at least there had been no more late-night visitors.

"The poor queen's not buried yet," Iras commented, crossing her arms under her ample bosom. "You mark Tryphaena's words. Berenike will make her move soon enough."

Apollodorus led the way through the crowds, his bronze helmet and sword glinting in the sunshine. The people of Alexandria were used to the comings and goings of royalty. They stepped aside so as not to impede the princess's progress but few turned their heads for long.

After a quarter of an hour they reached the main crossroads and turned into the Canopic Way, a broad avenue lined with the marble columns of grand houses. As they approached the temple dedicated to the Goddess Isis, Apollodorus called back, "Princess, would you like me to stop today?"

Before she could answer Cleopatra felt a sharp slap on her cheek. A rotten tomato tumbled down her front and oozed over her lap. Pips and stinking juice soaked her dress. Her face was stinging.

"That's what Rome will do to your father!" screamed her assailant.

"Oi! What do you think you're playing at?" Apollodorus shouted after the young man as he disappeared into the crowd.

Cleopatra was astonished. Nothing like this had ever happened to her before. She knew her father was so unpopular that he hardly dared venture into the town, but so far his daughters had been left alone. Hurriedly she wiped her face and toga. A sea of sullen faces watched her and yet no one had tried to stop the man. Not one person had stood up for a Ptolemy. It didn't bode well.

"Let's keep going, Apollodorus," she said.

She had never felt so unsafe in her own city.

"Princess, are you listening?" Diodorus rumbled.

Cleopatra was sitting at a desk in a large, airy room on the top floor of the Museion. Her teacher looked at her quizzically.

"Yes, yes, honestly I am."

But in truth she couldn't get the tomato incident out of her mind. The king had always had troubles – not enough money, poor harvests and Rome, their greedy neighbour, swallowing up kingdom after kingdom, never satisfied. Egypt was rich in wheat and gold, a tempting prize for such an empire, and for years the king had been paying ransoms to keep the Romans away. It wasn't popular with the people, but what else could he do? So why the tomato now?

"What was I lecturing you on, then?" asked her teacher, seeing that she was still not concentrating.

"On..." She thought for a moment. "On our lunar calendar. It's so accurate and superior that even the Romans are thinking of adopting it."

Diodorus's creased face broke into an amused smile. Even when distracted, Cleopatra was an excellent student.

"Well that's a reasonable summary I suppose. Can I suggest that next time you pay even closer attention? You missed out how our scholars calculated the length of the year. I don't want to have to repeat classes."

"Yes," sighed Cleopatra. She really did mean to give her studies the attention they deserved, for Diodorus was a famous scholar and it was an honour to be taught by such a man.

"Well, Princess, we'll finish the lesson here. I think our time is just about up."

As Cleopatra began to organize her notes, her thoughts returned to the incident. What had the man said when he threw the tomato? "That's what Rome will do to your father." The Romans were famous for humiliating kings they had deposed. They paraded them through the streets in cages while people threw rotten fruit, putrid meat, even rocks. Did the crowd think this was the fate that awaited her father?

There was a knock at the door. Diodorus got slowly to his feet.

"Ah, perfect timing. Here's Iras with your lunch. I'll see you tomorrow at the same hour. Strabus is lecturing you this afternoon. You know where his room is, don't you?"

Diodorus picked up his papyrus papers and a leather bag and nodded in Iras's direction. Many a scholar with his reputation would barely have acknowledged a servant, but he was unfailingly polite.

"I have to go, Iras. I must prepare an ointment of frankincense for one of my students. He has asthma and I think it might help."

"Yes, of course," said Iras. Diodorus was always trying out different compounds. "The honey poultice worked very well on my sore throat last week."

"Good, good," smiled the tutor, "I thought it would."

"I have news," said Iras, as soon as Diodorus left the room.

Cleopatra could tell she was excited.

"What is it?" she asked eagerly.

Iras lowered her voice.

"Do you think it's safe to talk here? Could there be spies from the palace? Tryphaena told you to be careful."

Iras was always worrying, but maybe she was right. Scholars came from all over the world to learn at the Museion. They looked like they were studying but who could tell?

"Let's go into the gardens," Cleopatra suggested.

Whatever it was Iras wanted to say, no one would be able to overhear them there.

9

IRAS pulled out two small loaves of bread and some cheese and figs from a bag. They were sitting on a bench in the shade of a sycamore tree well away from the students.

"What is it that you couldn't say inside?"

"Berenike has made her move. I heard it from a very reliable source." Iras paused and checked over her shoulder again. "One of her own maids."

"Those girls never speak," said Cleopatra. "They're too frightened."

"Well, Lysandra was so furious after the princess kicked a child slave, over and over, just for spilling some wine, I don't think she could help herself. She told me Berenike summoned your father and demanded he marry her. She said his support was ebbing away and that she alone could save him because she's so popular with the people of Alexandria. She might be a nightmare inside the palace, but Lysandra told me whenever she travels around the city she throws coins at the mob so they'll love her. She's insisting the announcement is made immediately after Queen Selene's funeral."

Things are moving too quickly, thought Cleopatra. Last

time she had seen Berenike she had been fawning over the king, not bossing him around. The funeral was only weeks away. There was very little time to stop her.

"She's awful," said Cleopatra, her green eyes flashing.

"I know. Lysandra said there was a big row. She even called your father 'the flute player'."

Cleopatra choked on her fig. She knew, of course, that Ptolemy was mockingly referred to in this way in the market place. The people of Alexandria despised his love of wine and music. But for his daughter to say it to his face was unbelievably disrespectful.

"I must get back to the palace to see if I can find out more," said Iras. "There's a rumour that the Romans are sniffing around Cyprus now. The island belongs to your father and it would be a humiliation if they took it."

Cleopatra stayed in the beautiful garden mulling over the news. Berenike was bad enough as a princess; if she became queen she would be a tyrant. Her father must see this. And then there was the question of the hated Romans. So far her father gave them enough each year in gold and wheat to satisfy them. It didn't make him popular, as taxes were high to pay for it, but it did stop them invading. But would a new marriage upset this delicate balance? Rome might think that Egypt under Berenike would be less easy to control. The more Cleopatra thought about it, the more confused she became. There were many possibilities but none of them seemed good.

That evening Apollodorus delivered a wooden board to Cleopatra. At last her sister had sent her a message. She read out loud, "The Museion gardens at midday tomorrow. Tryphaena."

"You won't be able to go," said Iras, who had just walked in. "A Roman ship came into the harbour this afternoon. They *have* invaded Cyprus. It's a disaster for your father. People are saying we'll be next, that the Romans will be here within the week, and they're blaming him. It's not safe outside the palace walls."

But Cleopatra hadn't seen Tryphaena since the night Queen Selene died. She had to go.

"I make the journey several times a week and there's never any trouble," she said, conveniently forgetting to mention the incident with the tomato.

"Well it won't be safe now," Iras answered. "Only yesterday I heard a man preaching to a crowd that the Ptolemys were secretly working with the Romans to strip this country of its wealth. And the crowd was applauding. I'm worried."

This only made Cleopatra even more determined to see her eldest sister.

"I must talk to Tryphaena. She'll know what to do."

She stood with her arms folded stubbornly across her chest until Iras relented, though only on the condition that the princess agreed to travel through the town in disguise.

And so the next morning Cleopatra walked through

Alexandria without guards for the first time in her life. Apollodorus wore a blue and green striped tunic and his fair hair was tucked under a head scarf. Cleopatra had only ever seen him in the red uniform of the palace guard and now he was transformed into a merchant, he was like a stranger. Apollodorus saw the look of shock on her face and pulled out a dagger he had hidden in the folds of his robe.

"Don't worry, I'm still a soldier," he laughed.

Iras dressed Cleopatra as his daughter. She plaited her curly hair into hundreds of tiny braids like any other local girl, changed her toga for a plain brown gown and put palm leaf sandals on her feet instead of the leather ones she usually wore. When Cleopatra looked at herself in the mirror she was startled by the change.

"Remember only to speak Egyptian," Iras said for the umpteenth time, giving her one last hug.

"Don't worry, we will," Cleopatra promised and with that she and Apollodorus disappeared into the crowded streets of Alexandria.

IRAS was making a fuss as usual, thought Cleopatra, as she went through the city with her guard. Although the roads were crowded, it was peaceful and she was elated to be walking so freely. They blended in perfectly, except for one thing: Apollodorus was too upright and correct. She nudged him.

"Stop marching," she said cheekily.

Apollodorus smiled.

"It's years of training. I'll try."

It was peculiar but now she was without an escort, she felt safe on the streets again. From time to time she paused to look at a stall or watch shoppers haggle. She found herself behind two young girls who must have been about her age, walking down the Canopic Way chatting and giggling. After a few paces they stopped and joined a small crowd watching a performing monkey. Cleopatra also slowed, captivated by their obvious delight in each other's company. For a moment she longed to join them. The royal children led such isolated lives, she wasn't even allowed to play with the children of the most senior courtiers.

Apollodorus interrupted her thoughts. "Come on. What would Iras think if she saw you daydreaming like this? She'd have a fit."

Twenty minutes later they arrived at the Museion gardens. Tryphaena was sitting on a stone bench by a pool full of blooming lotus flowers. She had chosen her position well, for there were no other seats near her and the young plants around provided no hiding places. Anyone loitering near enough to hear their conversation would be seen first.

"I hardly recognized you. What *are* you wearing?" asked Tryphaena as Cleopatra sat down on the bench. Cleopatra did her best to explain about Iras's worries but in truth she hardly recognized her sister and it wasn't because of her clothes; it was the transformation in her face. Tryphaena was usually so calm but now she looked pinched with great rings under her eyes and an anxious frown.

"Iras has a point," she said. "I take it that you've heard about Cyprus. I avoided the main routes on my way here and didn't have any problems but trouble often starts later in the day."

"Why did you want to see me?"

"Berenike's persuaded Father to marry her," Tryphaena said simply. "I wanted to say goodbye before I left."

"Why do you have to go?" asked Cleopatra. She couldn't bear the idea of her sister leaving. Tryphaena had always been a good friend to her and the palace could be such a lonely place.

"I can't stay," said Tryphaena sadly with her head bowed. "Think how it would be for me with Berenike as queen. Father is drinking more than ever and he won't be able to protect me."

Cleopatra knew it was true. Berenike would not miss a chance to humiliate her older sister, or worse.

"Where are you going?" she asked.

"I'm not sure. I'll have to leave Egypt. If I don't, Berenike will always worry that I could become a threat to her. I know what she's like."

The bitterness in Tryphaena's voice was unsettling.

"When are you going?"

"I'll be ready in about a week, but it would be better for you if I don't see you again. Have you been all right?"

"Yes. There's been nothing since the snake."

Tryphaena cradled Cleopatra's hands in her own.

"Good. Now that she's got her way I think she'll leave you alone. You're only a child after all. Just don't challenge her and you should be fine."

"Can I come with you?"

"No, but once I'm settled you could visit, if we can get the king to agree." The idea seemed to light up Tryphaena's face for a moment but then the clouds returned. "I have to be going. My guards think I'm borrowing a book from the library. If I stay too long they'll get suspicious. How are you getting home?"

"I'll go back the way I came."

Tryphaena stood up and then turned back to her younger sister.

"Hurry, then. I'm going to miss you."

"I'll miss you too," answered Cleopatra, but she held back her tears, not wanting to make their parting any more difficult than it already was.

Cleopatra walked slowly through the Museion gardens. They were so calm and peaceful, yet the future was so uncertain. What would Berenike do? Would Tryphaena be safe wherever she went? And what of her own future?

The path she had chosen wound through beds overflowing with flowers, drifting in the gentle breeze. Petals of dazzling pinks, yellows and reds contrasted with lush green leaves. Eventually she came to the magnificent entrance hall of the Museion, where she had agreed to meet Apollodorus. As she approached she could see that he was tense. He pointed at a stone vessel with a spout from which water was pouring steadily into a marble basin below.

"Princess, look at the clock," he said. 'When you left the water was up to here. Now look. It's almost empty."

"I'm sorry," she said, "but what's the hurry?"

"There's a demonstration in the town and it seems to be heading for the palace. I don't know how to get you back."

11

CLEOPATRA was surprised to see Apollodorus was so agitated. Normally Iras was the one in a panic.

"Did Tryphaena get back home?" she asked.

"She left ages ago. Hopefully she's ahead of the rabble. What have you been doing?"

"I went for a walk round the garden," she answered rather shamefacedly.

"The garden?" Apollodorus looked astonished. "At a time like this?"

He had every right to be cross. Tryphaena had told her to hurry home and yet she had wasted time.

"Listen," he said. "A crowd is marching on the palace. The guards will hold them off, but then there's bound to be a riot in the city. We've got to get you behind the walls without you being spotted."

"Nobody noticed us on the way." Cleopatra was surprised at how calm she felt. "Why don't we just join the crowd and then separate off when we get close to home."

"I think you're right," said Apollodorus. "There's no other way. Speak only in Egyptian, stay close to me and do exactly as I say."

They walked down the Museion steps and into the

Canopic Way. On the way the pavements had been full. Now the street vendors, fortune tellers and musicians had melted away and across the street a barber was boarding up his shop.

A group of people surged past them, walking briskly towards a demonstration that could now be heard in the distance.

"Let's catch up," whispered Apollodorus. "There's safety in numbers. Who knows, we might even get to the front and overtake the march."

They joined the growing crowd. As they got closer the size of the gathering took Cleopatra's breath away. Hundreds and hundreds of people were risking their lives marching on the palace. There were bakers, servants, butchers, beggars, metal workers and farmers who must have come into the city for the day and they were all angry with her father. Thank goodness none of them realized that his daughter was among them.

A chant went up ahead of them.

"No more grain to Rome! The flute player must go!"

The people around her took it up.

"No more grain to Rome! The flute player must go!"

The sound was deafening.

More people poured into the streets. Cleopatra held tightly onto Apollodorus's hand, worried that she might be pulled away from him as the crowd surged in one direction and then another. They reached the large square at the intersection of the Argeus Boulevard and the Canopic Way. Ahead were the high walls of the palace, but between them and the gates was this huge crowd, which was now slowing down to listen to a speaker.

A young man climbed onto a hastily arranged platform by a fountain.

"Today and every day," he cried, "hundreds of sacks of grain are being loaded onto boats at the docks here in Alexandria. That grain was grown in Egypt but will it be eaten by Egyptians?"

"No!" shouted the crowd.

"That's right. It's going to Rome, our enemy. Rome, that has just taken Cyprus from us. And what does our king do? He feeds his enemy and starves his own people. Can that be right?"

"No!" roared every person around Cleopatra.

"Egyptians all over this land are working hard, but is the king?" cried the speaker above the noise. "Our dykes, which should have been repaired in time for the coming floods, are falling apart. It's the king's job to maintain them. That's why we pay our taxes, and he hasn't done it. We need a new king!"

The crowd cheered in response.

Cleopatra was mesmerized. She'd never heard her father criticized in public before. What was he going to do? And what if the speaker was right? Did Egypt need a new leader? She was in turmoil, torn between loyalty to her father and doubt about his wisdom as a ruler. In her confusion she turned to Apollodorus, but he wasn't there. He must have been pulled away while she was listening to that wretched speaker. And now she was all alone in an angry crowd.

ISIS, *help me*, thought Cleopatra. *But I mustn't panic. Apollodorus must be around here somewhere.*

She craned her neck, trying to look in all directions, but she was so much shorter than everyone else that it was impossible to see any distance. All the men were dressed in the sort of clothes that Apollodorus was wearing. How was she going to tell him apart?

She was tempted to pull the hand of the nearest man and say, "Help me. I've lost my servant." But that might give her away. She could pretend Apollodorus was her father, but what if the stranger recognized her? Or even if he didn't, what would she say her name was and where would she say she lived? It was hopeless. She would just have to find him. She searched again frantically but all the time the crowd was surging this way and that and Apollodorus might be being pulled further and further away from her.

I'll never find him like this, she thought.

Slowly she began threading herself through the crowd in the direction of the palace, forcing her way into the tiniest gaps. Occasionally she looked up and was relieved to see the great gates looming larger and larger. She didn't know what she would do when she got there as they were firmly shut but at least she was getting closer to home.

The speaker finished and climbed down from the platform and another took the stage. Cleopatra sighed with relief. They were holding the crowd's attention. Once they'd finished she wasn't sure what would happen. Maybe they would try to storm the palace. Before that she wanted to be safe inside, behind the familiar line of soldiers.

Slight as she was, she kept weaving her way through the crush. The crowd was thinning a little and the palace gates were only a hundred yards or so away.

She pushed past two fat men, so alike they must be brothers. Both were dressed in long, flowing robes with purple turbans. Just as she got beyond them she felt a hand grab the back of her neck.

"Hey, what are you doing, shoving everyone? A child your age shouldn't be at a meeting like this," shouted one of the men in a foreign accent as he pulled her back towards him with a firm grip.

"I'm sorry," said Cleopatra nervously.

"She's probably a pickpocket," said the other. "There's bound to be loads of them about."

"I'm not!"

"I'd check your things if I were you," the man carried on. "You said she pushed past you. That's their way of distracting you while they take your money."

Cleopatra was passed to the second man who took a

strong grip of her wrist.

"I'm not a thief," she pleaded. "I'm searching for my father. We got caught up in the crowd on the way home and now we've been separated."

As she spoke the first man patted his robes all over, looking for something.

"My god, she's robbed me!" he shouted. "My purse has gone. I had five bits of silver in it."

"I haven't taken anything. Please," begged Cleopatra, "I haven't got your money. You can search me." She pulled futilely at her brown tunic trying to prove that she had nothing hidden.

"Oh, you're going to get a beating my girl. I'll see to that when I get you to the market official. Do you want a taste of the mud now?"

The man thrust her face down into the dust on the square floor. She felt her lip split as he pushed her into the ground. Then he yanked her up again.

"Where's my money?" he shouted straight into her face. Spit sprayed across her cheeks.

Her dress was covered in grime, her hair was tussled and blood was seeping from the crack in her lip. Even if she told him who she was he'd never believe that she was a princess, the daughter of King Ptolemy. But what else could she do?

"STOP that."

Out of the crowd, as if by a miracle, stepped Apollodorus.

Cleopatra wriggled free, relief surging through her.

"Are you the father of this thief?" asked the fat man.

"I'm her father, but don't you dare call her that."

"I'm telling you, I felt her take my money. I grabbed her as soon as I felt it."

"Then where is it now?" asked Apollodorus simply.

"She probably dropped it," answered Cleopatra's accuser. "As soon as she felt my hand on her neck she'd have hidden it in the dirt."

"How much was it?"

"Five pieces of silver."

"Here's ten, now let her go."

The man reluctantly handed her over. "You're lucky!" he shouted after them. "Next time she'll get a hundred lashes if I have anything to do with it."

Apollodorus grabbed Cleopatra tightly by the upper arm and marched her towards the gate and then beyond it to a side street that ran the length of the palace. She could tell he was both relieved and furious, and she could imagine the lecture he and Iras were going to give her that evening. Still, anything was better than being caught outside in a riot.

Halfway along the narrow street was a small door cut into the wall. It was a servant's entrance. Apollodorus knocked gently. The door opened an inch or two. They were home.

Iras was horrified when she heard what had happened.

"That's it," she said, dabbing Cleopatra's swollen lip with ointment, "you must stay in the palace until things calm down. I can't bear to think of what might have happened to you."

Iras was tight-lipped and tense all afternoon and her anxiety grew that evening as she tidied up. They could hear the distant rumble of what sounded like a street battle. General Achillas had ordered that all the shutters be bolted so they could only guess at what was happening outside. Each time a stone whistled past the window or they heard a crash, Iras jumped up and ran to the door where Apollodorus – now back in uniform – stood guard. He told them what he had heard from passing soldiers – that the demonstrators had tried to storm the palace walls but had been easily repelled. In their frustration they had turned to looting. That was the sound they could hear, but there was really nothing to worry about.

"Thank goodness the soldiers have kept them away," said Iras. "But what about next time?"

"Next time it will be the same," Apollodorus reassured her. "The king is surrounded by loyal troops. You'll see."

As he spoke, Cleopatra studied her guard carefully. His expression was normally easy to read but now he looked wary. She wanted to believe what he said but deep down inside she knew that this was different – the palace had never been stormed before. And Apollodorus wouldn't want to tell Iras the full story in front of her. She was desperate to see for herself what was really happening outside. The only way was to open her shutters but Iras would never go against an order from General Achillas. She had to have the room to herself.

She stretched theatrically and shook the plaits out of her curly hair.

"Iras, I'm exhausted," she said. "I'm going to go to bed early tonight."

"I'm not surprised after the day you've had," said her nurse sympathetically. "But are you sure your lip is all right? Do you want one of Diodorus's sleeping draughts to help with the pain?"

"No honestly, it doesn't hurt that much. It's just a small cut."

She couldn't wait for Iras to go but she knew not to hurry her; her nurse would only get suspicious. So she lay down, pulled the linen sheet up to her chin, yawned and began to breathe slowly and deeply, the way she imagined she would when asleep.

At last Iras finished her chores and Cleopatra had the room to herself. She lay still for several minutes more in case Iras came back for something, and then she crept out of bed and tiptoed to the window. Carefully, she slid the bolts and pushed open the wooden shutters. The left one squeaked loudly. She stopped, her ears straining for any sound of footsteps. There was none. She pushed again, wincing as it creaked open.

Below her was the comforting silhouette of the thick palace walls but beyond was a city in turmoil. Fires burned all over the town. In the nearest streets they illuminated crowds baying at lines of her father's soldiers. The guards were standing in rows holding up painted shields to protect themselves from the missiles that were being hurled at them. An officer was shouting "Hold firm" as rocks and stones thudded down. Then a young soldier was hit in the head. Blood streamed down his face. Horrified, Cleopatra watched him stagger and fall out of sight. How many more people would be injured or even killed tonight?

A cloud of dense smoke hung in the air and burnt the back of her throat. She swallowed hard and it made her cough.

A rock suddenly whizzed by and smashed on the stone wall just beyond her window. She jumped back as a fragment broke off and skated across the marble floor.

This can't go on, she thought as she hastily closed the shutters. Never mind the Romans. The people of

Alexandria were invading and the king had to do something before it was too late.

APOLLODORUS came into the apartment early in the morning looking relieved. He reported that the looters had been dispersed at dawn and the army had taken control of Alexandria once more. He also brought news of an order sent by the king to each of the royal children. They were to stay within the palace walls and must be accompanied at all times by a guard. Cleopatra couldn't even go to her lessons at the Museion.

For five long days she was confined to the palace. Diodorus arranged for work to be sent and a servant arrived every afternoon with a leather satchel containing the next day's lessons and collected the exercises she had already completed. Cleopatra spent most mornings working but she found it hard to concentrate on geometry, philosophy or history when everything was so unsettled. To make matters worse she hadn't heard from Tryphaena since the riots and she hadn't seen her father since the death of Queen Selene. Usually he would send for her at least once a week and she would go to his private rooms where he would ask her about her school work or get her to read to him. Too often the king had a glass of wine in his hand and a muddled look in his eyes, but at least if he summoned her she could ask him what was going on.

Iras could see that Cleopatra was frustrated.

"Your father will call for you soon," she said. "He's busy. I walk through the city most days and I can feel that the people could turn again at any time. He must be making plans in case they do."

All the uncertainty was making Cleopatra restless. She felt she would explode if she spent another hour in her room with just her studies for company.

"I've got an idea," she said that lunchtime. "I'm going to climb the palace ramparts this afternoon. I've never done it before."

"Apollodorus must go with you. It's the king's orders," said Iras firmly. "You're not to go anywhere alone."

Cleopatra knew there was no point arguing.

The ramparts were over ten feet wide and built of sandstone. The staircase Cleopatra and Apollodorus climbed brought them to the eastern wall. Below them on the right was Alexandria's busy Jewish quarter, scarred with charred buildings from the night of the riots. On the left was the main palace courtyard.

As soon as she stepped out into the spring sunshine Cleopatra's spirits rose.

"It's fantastic, Apollodorus," she said. "I don't know why I've never come before. Have you ever been up here?"

"Yes, Princess. Many years ago I worked up here," he answered. He pointed at the soldiers that stood every twenty yards along the wall, facing out towards the city. "I was one of those sentries when I first came to the palace."

"Why did you change jobs?"

The merest frown made her aware that he was uncomfortable with the conversation.

"Your mother requested it, over ten years ago. I became her personal bodyguard and then later yours."

"Why did she choose you?"

"There was an assassination attempt; a madman tried to stab the queen. I was one of the soldiers that protected her."

"You saved her life?"

"Yes," Apollodorus said quietly.

Now Cleopatra understood. He was a modest man who never boasted. Still, he should be proud of what he'd done.

"Is that why Father rewarded you with a medal?" She pointed at a gold badge pinned to his tunic. "You're the only guard I've ever seen wearing one of those."

Apollodorus nodded.

"Why is it shaped like a fly?"

"It's supposed to signify that however many times the wearer gets swatted away he will always return."

As they talked, they walked towards a corner of the ramparts where the palace walls turned and skirted along the seashore. Below was the royal port. It was full of ships, their coloured sails and flags dancing in the breeze, but they were small craft, fit only for touring the country on the rivers and canals. Her father's magnificent ocean-going vessel, built from wood imported from Lebanon, was missing.

"Where's Father's boat? Is it being refitted?" Cleopatra asked.

Apollodorus scanned the distant boatbuilders' wharfs in the two main harbours on either side of the tall lighthouse.

"I can't see it," he said, squinting into the sunshine. "Wait! Look! Isn't that it there?" He pointed out to sea and right on the edge of the horizon Cleopatra could just make out a large vessel with purple sails and a flag at the tip of its mast.

"That's odd," she said. "Why would it be sailing without him?"

The king's ship only set sail when her father visited foreign kings or governments. He would leave with a great fanfare. His ship would be blessed, soldiers would salute and the whole court would come and wave as the boat floated into the open sea. Cleopatra had witnessed many such occasions. Surely she would know if the king was leaving on a voyage.

A sudden noise in the courtyard below distracted her. Hundreds of soldiers were pouring out of their barracks. More came running through the gates.

"That's General Achillas, isn't it?" said Cleopatra. "And look, there's Father's priest, Pshereni, behind him."

Both men were shouting and gesticulating frantically. From this height they looked like demented ants.

"Let's get back to your rooms," said Apollodorus. "Something's not right."

"TAKE me to Tryphaena," ordered Cleopatra.

"Princess, I don't think you should be wandering around now," pleaded Apollodorus. "Not until we're sure it's safe. Who knows what General Achillas and Pshereni are up to. They've always been close to Princess Berenike. I don't trust them."

They were arguing on the rampart walls at the top of a steep staircase.

"I've got to see my sister," said Cleopatra stubbornly, hands on hips and green eyes blazing. "I'm fed up with waiting in that apartment, never knowing what's going on."

Apollodorus gave a worried sigh.

"It's too dangerous. Tryphaena told you to stay away, didn't she? For your own good."

Cleopatra was past caring.

"If you don't take me, I'll go by myself – but I am not going back to my rooms."

She had a determined look that Apollodorus had seen many times before. He knew that she was not to be reasoned with.

"All right, we'll go," he said in a more conciliatory tone. "But Princess please, give me a moment to think how to get you there without meeting anyone on the way." He paused, as if remembering something, then smiled. "Follow me."

He led her down a twisting staircase that opened onto a wide corridor with painted columns on either side. They had only gone ten yards when he pulled her behind a pillar. There she was surprised to see a low, wooden door, painted the same pale yellow as the stone walls and so well camouflaged that she had never noticed it before. Apollodorus pushed her through, shutting it quickly behind them.

"What are you doing?" she called out in the darkness.

"Hold on, I'm counting, three bricks across and twelve bricks up ... ah, here it is."

Cleopatra heard him strike a flint. Sparks flew and then a flame began to burn on the wick of an oil lamp.

"Thank the gods," Apollodorus said softly as he took several deep breaths. In the flickering light Cleopatra could see that he was sweating.

They were in a tall, narrow passage. On either side were stone slab walls. They were unplastered and had no paintings or mosaics. The floor felt dry and dusty underfoot which was unusual, for the palace was kept spotlessly clean by an army of slaves.

"Where are we?" Cleopatra asked.

"It's a disused corridor," answered Apollodorus. "I found it one day, many years ago before you were born, when I was ordered to help search the palace because someone was stealing from the kitchens. I used to come here when I wanted time to myself, just to sit and think. I've always left a flint and lamp at each of the entrances."

"Where does it go to?"

"In one direction it comes out in the palace wall near the coast. The other entrance is about a hundred yards from the king's rooms. That's why I brought you here. Tryphaena's rooms are close by."

"It's strange there are no other doors."

"I know. It was probably built as an escape route in case there was ever any trouble. Now follow me carefully. The floor isn't good in places."

Together they walked gingerly forward. Cleopatra soon lost all sense of direction. She felt that she was mainly walking in a straight line but then the path began to descend quite steeply. As they got lower the air smelt damp and the flagstones were cold. The passage levelled out and then gently climbed again. She began to feel claustrophobic. The stale air felt as if nobody had breathed it for a hundred years. What if a sudden breeze blew out the lamp? What if the ceiling fell in? In places she noticed stones on the ground that must have fallen over the years.

"How much further is it?" she said.

"Just to the top of this slope."

They walked on and on.

"We're here," said Apollodorus at last. "I'm going to blow out the lamp, so nobody sees the light as I open the door."

Once again Cleopatra waited.

"Apollodorus, what are you doing?" she whispered, trying not to let her nerves show in her voice.

"I'm putting the flint back. Shush, I've got to listen. This door comes out on one of the main corridors. We don't want to bump into anybody."

They waited another long moment, then to her relief she heard him tug the latch and they slipped through the doorway.

"Quick! Round to the left."

Together they hugged the walls of a wide corridor, turned the corner and walked smack into General Achillas.

"Good afternoon, Princess," he leered, "and what do you think you are doing here?"

CLEOPATRA stood open mouthed. General Achillas was the last person she wanted to run into. Behind him were two guards standing either side of the great bronze doors of the king's room, but they were Berenike's soldiers. What on earth were they doing there? She had no time to think before Achillas pushed Apollodorus aside and came closer. He leant down until his thick lips were level with her ears and barked straight at her.

"I said, what are you doing here?"

She could feel his hot breath on her neck. Achillas had never spoken to her like this before. What was going on? She resolved not to give him the satisfaction of seeing how alarmed she was and, looking straight ahead, answered haughtily, "I don't believe a princess needs your permission to walk around the palace."

"Then I'm afraid that you're going to have to get used to a few changes."

Cleopatra tried to control her temper and with as steady a voice as she could manage said, "And what are those, General?"

"Come and see Princess Berenike. She'll tell you."

Cleopatra turned automatically in the direction of

Berenike's rooms.

"Not that way," laughed Achillas cruelly.

He pointed towards the king's apartment. Now Cleopatra understood. Berenike's soldiers outside the king's doors, Achillas's insolent manner, and the boat on the horizon ... it all added up. Berenike had made her move. King Ptolemy the Twelfth was king no more.

Achillas marched Cleopatra through the bronze doors into an ornate chamber. Inside, anxious looking courtiers were milling around. In the middle stood Berenike caressing her leopard cub, Nefer, and talking animatedly with Pshereni. Cleopatra was horrified; her sister was already wearing her father's crown. Made from solid gold worked into the shape of a serpent, it was only supposed to be worn by the rightful monarch and Berenike could never be that while her father was alive. Around her arms were gold bands. *Those were meant for Queen Selene's tomb*, thought Cleopatra, instantly recognizing the bangles.

Achillas pulled her towards her sister.

"Pshereni, come. All you others get out," ordered Berenike.

Cleopatra's heart sank. Pshereni, her father's priest, must be a traitor as well.

"Look what I found wandering around the palace," said Achillas once the courtiers had left. He laughed as he pushed Cleopatra forward. Berenike showed no surprise. She coolly surveyed her sister, tickling Nefer under the chin all the while. The leopard purred gently.

"Where did you find her, Achillas?" asked Pshereni.

"Just outside."

"How did she get that close? I thought you had patrols throughout the palace."

"We do," Achillas answered, with less swagger than before. "I don't know how she got here without being stopped. But I'll find out, don't worry. No doubt Apollodorus had something to do with it."

"Don't squabble, you two," said Berenike. She turned to Cleopatra. "So what do you want?" she asked coldly.

Cleopatra had to think quickly. She couldn't answer honestly or she'd get Tryphaena in trouble, so instead she said, "I came to see Father to find out what was going on. I saw his ship sailing from the ramparts."

Berenike circled around her menacingly.

"The coward has left Egypt. As you can see, I am now in charge."

"When's he coming back?" asked Cleopatra.

"Never," said her sister. "No doubt he'll drink himself to death in some Roman tavern. I am now your queen."

The king had gone to Rome. Is that what Berenike was saying? But wasn't Rome his enemy? Cleopatra couldn't understand it. If only she could talk to her elder sister.

"What about Tryphaena?" she said. "Where is she?"

"Ah," said Berenike, "I have sad news. Our sister died

this morning. She ate fish that was poorly prepared. I was just discussing the funeral arrangements with Pshereni."

Pshereni smiled a thin smile and put a bony arm around Cleopatra's shoulder.

"I'm sorry, my dear."

Cleopatra had never seen a man look less sorry in her life. Just having his arm around her made her skin crawl. She felt the blood rushing to her brain. Berenike had spoken in such a matter-of-fact way, as if she were telling her of the death of a family dog, not their own sister. She wasn't even pretending to be sad. And now this priest as well. They were all in it together, Berenike, Achillas and Pshereni, of that she was sure, but now was not the time to make accusations. Berenike had already demonstrated just how ruthless she could be.

"How sad," she said quietly. "I shall miss her."

"Yes, I'm sure we all will," said Berenike perfunctorily. "But I also have some happy news that should help us get over our loss. I have summoned everyone to the throne room at sunset tomorrow to announce the date of my coronation. Pshereni will be leading the celebratory prayers."

"Whatever you wish," murmured Cleopatra.

"That is what I wish," retorted Berenike, her blue eyes flashing with anger. "But I want more than that from you. I will require that you swear allegiance to your new queen. Our sister Arsinoe will also attend along with our brothers and they will do likewise. Do you understand?"

"Yes."

Cleopatra understood perfectly. Berenike wanted a show of family unity to help her secure the throne. Had Tryphaena refused to play her part? Was that why she'd been killed? She remembered Tryphaena's last warning. Stay loyal to the king. But he had gone to Egypt's enemy. She didn't know which way to turn. Everything was so confusing and now she had lost a true friend who would have been able to guide her.

"Cleopatra, I'm warning you, I don't want any trouble," said Berenike. "If you cause me any difficulties I'll feed you to Nefer, bit by bit. Do I make myself understood? Now return to your rooms and wait there until you get more instructions."

17

"THANK Isis you're back," gasped Iras. "Every time I let you out of my sight something happens." She looked close to tears.

"Have you heard the news?" Cleopatra asked.

"I told her," said Apollodorus.

"I don't understand. Why is Father going to Rome?"

"One of the guards just told me," answered Apollodorus. "The riot ten days ago, when you were at the Museion with Tryphaena, convinced the king that marrying Berenike wouldn't help him. He's decided that he needs reinforcements."

"He's gone to Rome to bring soldiers here?" said Cleopatra. "But the Romans took Cyprus from us. They're our enemies. Why would he do that?"

"They're the only power strong enough to help him."

"But why would they?" Cleopatra was still bewildered.

"For money. Your father will promise them even more gold and grain. If they believe him, they might reinstate him."

"But sending even more food to Rome isn't going to make him more popular."

"If he can persuade Rome to send enough soldiers, he won't have to worry about how popular he is," Apollodorus said dryly.

"How long will all this take?" asked Iras.

"Well, it will take him forty days, at least, to get to Rome," said Apollodorus, "and then there's the job of persuading the Senate to raise an army. It could be many months."

"And he might not be successful," said Cleopatra quietly. As she spoke, her knees gave way and she sank down onto a low wooden chair. For a moment she didn't care about Egypt and its problems. She felt overwhelmed at the thought that she'd been abandoned. Tryphaena was dead and her father hadn't even said goodbye.

Iras knelt down beside her, put a comforting arm round her shoulders and said, "What are we going to do, Apollodorus?"

"Look," he answered, "we can't know when the king will be back but I'm certain he will be one day. He'll do anything to return and in the meantime you and I will protect the princess."

Cleopatra thought about her father. He had weaknesses; they were all too apparent. But he was also resilient and tough. How else had he fought for all these years to keep his throne when Rome had swallowed up country after country around him? He wouldn't give it up easily. But until her father returned, she had to make plans of her own.

"Iras, Apollodorus, I need to get away, just as Tryphaena

wanted to," said Cleopatra. "But she left it too late. I don't want to make the same mistake. Berenike doesn't trust me and I'm only useful to her until tomorrow night when she announces her coronation. After that she could turn on me at any time. Look how brutally she dealt with Tryphaena. I don't believe that bad fish story for a moment and neither do you."

"I know," said Iras, "but we can't just go running off into the night."

"I am not going to swear loyalty to Berenike," said Cleopatra. "Not while the king is still alive. It's not right. I've got to leave before tomorrow—"

"Iras, maybe there is sense in what the princess says," interrupted Apollodorus. "Berenike is preoccupied with plans for her coronation. This might be the easiest time to disappear."

"But where can we take her?" said Iras in dismay. "I wouldn't trust any of the noble families to shelter her. They would barter her for more land."

"I agree. She'll have to disappear completely," said Apollodorus.

"How can a princess vanish in Alexandria?"

"She can't. But she could hide deep in the country down the Nile. We know that she can pass as a native Egyptian. Cleopatra must go to Upper Egypt. There we can keep her safe."

THEY left the palace early next morning, dressed as peasants. Iras hurried Cleopatra into the most crowded markets in the city. Berenike would, in all probability, be searching everywhere for them and they would only be safe if they could disappear unnoticed into the busy streets.

"Is Apollodorus going to meet us later?" whispered Cleopatra as they hurried along.

"No. When you were asleep, we decided that I would take you south to Bahri, my family village. It's a quiet place. Apollodorus is so fair he would stand out a mile, but thankfully with your dark colouring you'll blend in."

"But what will happen to him? He can't go back to the palace."

"He'll be fine," said Iras. "Apollodorus is resourceful. Think how easily he sneaked us out, right under Berenike's nose."

"It was the same passage he used to get me to the king's rooms yesterday," said Cleopatra. "He told me then that he thought it was an old escape route." She paused and then said, "Iras, you've both risked so much for me—"

"Now don't you worry about that," interrupted Iras. "And keep your eyes to the ground. I don't want anyone recognizing you."

Cleopatra tried to do as she was told but occasionally she couldn't help looking up. She thought she knew Alexandria but now, away from the wide avenues, she realized how mistaken she was. Iras was leading her through narrow lanes lined with mud houses. Unlike the broad, paved streets that she was used to, these had floors of packed earth and she had to watch where she stepped, for in places rotting food was piling up and dirty water formed stinking puddles. It was hard to recognize her city in this quarter.

They were heading away from the coast towards Lake Mareotis, which was linked by a short canal to the River Nile. All they had with them were two baskets woven from palm leaves. One contained a tunic each and a sheet and blanket. The other, a pot and a water gourd. There was no room for anything else.

"Apollodorus reckons Berenike will think you're trying to join the king in Rome. The guards will search the sea ports before they look anywhere else."

Cleopatra realized that Iras was trying to reassure her. *I hope you're right*, she thought. The idea of being dragged back to Berenike was unbearable.

Twenty minutes later they arrived at the lake. The shore was lined with boats. Some were large, seaworthy crafts with great sails and masts but most were made from lashed papyrus reeds and were fit only for the river. Cleopatra and Iras checked the banks for the red uniform of the palace soldiers.

"I think we've done it." Cleopatra smiled broadly at her nurse, relief flooding through her.

"I won't be happy until we've set sail," Iras answered. "Come on."

Together they climbed down the slippery stone steps to the water's edge, dodging dockers who were heaving sacks of grain from boats to waiting carts.

Iras peered this way and that, trying to choose a boatman. North or south, the journey was of predictable length. The boats rowed with the current one way and were blown by the prevailing winds the other. Iras estimated that it would take around twelve days to get to Bahri so she wanted to find a captain who looked trustworthy and a deck that was clean. But most of all she wanted a boat that was ready to leave.

Quickly she picked one and they reached the boat just as the last sack was lifted from its deck. It was wide with a high prow and stern, a steering oar at the back and at its centre a tall mast, which held a linen sail. The captain was short and stocky. He wore a baggy, white, linen robe tied around his waist. As they approached, he smiled. His teeth were worn and several were missing.

"Are you travelling to Dendera?" Iras asked.

"I'm going further than that. All the way to Nubia."

"Would you have room for me and my daughter?"

The man looked them both up and down and replied, "How much?"

Iras got down to the business of haggling and in no time the deal was done.

"The boat is setting sail at midday," she reported to Cleopatra. "The captain says he's got to get paid for the wheat, buy some salt to take back downriver and then he'll get going. I think we're likely to be his only passengers, although he does have a helper with him, a boy from the south."

"Did you get a good price?"

"I think so. I got him down by agreeing to do all the cooking. Now let's go back to the last market we saw and get some food for the trip. Oh, and I told the captain that you were called Mayum."

"Why?" Cleopatra asked.

"Well I couldn't very well say your name, could I? You must now be an Egyptian at all times and remember to call me 'Mother'."

"I will, but why Mayum?"

"Because she was my best friend when I was a girl. It was the first name that came into my head. Now, come on, we've got things to do."

Iras bought barley, onions, garlic and beans. The grocer weighed everything meticulously, balancing it carefully against copper weights. Iras tapped her foot impatiently. They needed to be getting on.

"Right, now all we need is some bread. Let's go over there." She pointed to a baker's stall in the corner of the square.

A woman with a baby strapped to her back was ahead of them in the queue. She was taking forever to choose a loaf. She picked up each one and squeezed and smelt it.

"Are you sure it's fresh?" she kept demanding.

Iras was getting edgy. She called out over the woman's shoulder to the baker, "Could we have six loaves, please? As soon as you can."

Suddenly Cleopatra saw four guards at the far corner of the square. She watched them spread out and begin to patrol each stall, staring at face after face. They must be from the palace. She discreetly tugged Iras's dress. Iras saw the red of the uniform, grabbed the bread, tossed the baker a coin and they hurried away.

"That was too close," she said as they walked briskly through a narrow lane back to the lake, "I pray that boat is ready to go. We need to get out of here."

They walked past the last mud house. The lake shimmered in front of them but they couldn't see their boat anywhere.

"Oh Isis, he's left without us," muttered Iras. "And there are soldiers everywhere. What are we going to do now?"

CLEOPATRA looked along the banks of the lake, her heart pumping loudly in her chest. Soldiers were searching the hold of a boat that was only yards away. They were shouting at its captain, cutting open sacks of grain and stabbing bundles of hay with pitchforks. On the next boat a sailor pleaded in vain for his cargo not to be destroyed.

Cleopatra and Iras joined the crowd on the quayside.

"How are we going to get out of this?" Iras whispered.

Hearing the panic in her voice, Cleopatra desperately looked in the other direction, searching for somewhere, anywhere, they could hide. And there, in the distance, she saw the boat they were supposed to be on, drifting along in the gentle breeze. They must have missed it by only minutes.

"Iras, look! That's our boat isn't it?" she whispered.

Iras looked doubtful.

"It could be. They all look alike to me. Anyway, who cares? It's gone."

Cleopatra looked again and saw that its sails were drooping and it was making hardly any progress. She had an idea.

"Let's go after it. I think we can catch up and we can't

go on another. They're all being searched."

"It's impossible," said Iras. "If we run the soldiers will spot us."

"I know. Let's walk along the towpath. There are so many people, they won't notice. We can run when we're out of sight."

They walked as fast as they could without attracting attention, turning to check every now and then to see where the soldiers were. They were moving slowly along the bank, stopping at every boat and searching it. As the distance between them and their pursuers grew, Cleopatra relaxed a little. Now they had to catch up and get the captain's attention, and they had to risk running or they'd never do it. Praying that the wind would not pick up and carry the boat off, she grabbed Iras's hand.

"Come on."

Cleopatra ran easily, her young legs swiftly covering the ground, but Iras was much older, and she was plump as well. They had gone no distance before she was panting badly; Cleopatra dragged her along. A loaf and some beans bounced out of the basket but they didn't stop. Her own lungs were beginning to ache from the effort, but they were closing the gap. She could distinctly see the captain tidying a rope. It was definitely the right boat. She glanced behind, praying that nobody was following. She checked again, then shouted at the top of her voice.

"Hey, it's Iras and Mayum! Come back!"

The captain didn't seem to hear but the young boy at the other end of the vessel pointed at them. The captain waved and steered the boat over to the water's edge.

"Thank Isis," said Iras breathlessly. "I couldn't have taken another step."

Just then an arrow screeched through the air and stabbed into the ground only a foot ahead of them. They both spun round.

Not ten yards away a soldier emerged from the tall rushes that lined the river. His bow was taut as he pointed another arrow at them.

"Where are you going in such a hurry?"

Before they could answer, he blew a shrill whistle that could be heard the length of the river. In the distance more soldiers came running.

20

"LET me ask you again," said a sergeant, "why were you running away?"

He was an ugly man, made uglier by a boil on his left cheek, which had swollen up. Cleopatra could hardly bear to look at him.

"I've already told you," answered Iras. "I was trying to catch up with the boat. We came to Alexandria to sell cloth and now we need to get back for a wedding in Dendera. I could see that we might be held up for hours at the docks. When I saw the boat in the distance, I thought it would be quicker to catch up than wait for another. That's all."

Iras and Cleopatra were being interrogated on the river bank. They were sitting on damp grass surrounded by a ring of soldiers. The boatman and his boy had been rounded up as well.

"And you," said the sergeant. "Why did you bother to come back if, as you say, you'd never met them before today?"

"I wish I hadn't," said the captain sulkily, "but I felt bad that I'd left earlier than arranged and I thought it was only right to stop. I don't know anything about them, I promise."

The sergeant went over to his officer and reported the conversation again.

Cleopatra, Iras, the captain and the boy sat in silence. Iras was chewing her nails distractedly. The sun was now high in the sky. The soldiers were obviously suspicious but they had no way of knowing whether they had caught the missing princess or a couple of peasants. None of them were from the palace barracks so they couldn't tell. Cleopatra could only pray that Iras would somehow convince them. It wasn't much of a plan but what else could they do?

Eventually the officer came over and said to Iras, "The girl you say is your daughter is the same age as the one we are looking for. She also fits the description – her hair is dark and her eyes green."

"But, Sir, there must be hundreds of girls in Alexandria like that," pleaded Iras, "and because of that I will miss my sister's wedding."

"You were caught running away. I have instructions not to let anyone who is behaving suspiciously leave the city. I have sent for someone from the palace who can identify the girl. Then we will know."

Iras began to sob. Cleopatra knew her tears were caused by fear rather than grief. It was hopeless. She was sure to be recognized. Anyone who knew her would instantly see through the peasant disguise. And then what? Berenike would not be forgiving, of that she was certain.

"Can I go?" asked the captain. "I've got nothing to do with this, Sir."

"No. I need to be sure that you were not involved in a plot as well."

The captain rolled his eyes disbelievingly.

"How long is this going to take?"

"I don't know. As you can imagine, anyone that knows the princess is being used to try and identify her. As soon as someone is free, they will come. Now sit down and shut up."

They waited in a huddle. Cleopatra slowly felt her fear turn to resignation. Berenike had won again. There was nothing to be done.

"You, get up! The palace has finally sent someone."

The sun was low in the sky. They had all spent the day on the riverbank with no food or water but Cleopatra wasn't hungry. All she could think about was what awaited her and how much trouble Iras would be in.

They stood up. The sergeant with the swollen cheek grabbed Cleopatra, hurting her as he squeezed her arm unnecessarily hard.

"Over here."

Her eyes locked with Iras's as she was pulled out of the ring of soldiers. Would she ever see her nurse again?

The sergeant pulled her along the towpath as a horse came galloping towards them. This must be the person who would unmask her.

The horse slowed to a trot but Cleopatra still couldn't see who it was as a hood covered the rider's face. The horse pulled up and the man climbed stiffly down and pulled back his cloak. It was her teacher, Diodorus. Cleopatra groaned. He would recognize her in anything.

"Please could you bring this animal some oats and water," said Diodorus to the officer. "Now where is the runaway princess?"

"Here," said the soldier, tugging the back of Cleopatra's curly hair so that her face was pulled up ready for inspection.

"Right, let me have a good look. I've been doing this all day and I'm getting tired. Please could you turn towards the sun?"

Diodorus studied her intently.

"Officer, I'm done," he said at last.

"Well?" asked the soldier.

"I've never seen her before in my life."

Cleopatra was dumbstruck.

"She's just a peasant girl unlucky enough to be stopped because of all the fuss at the palace. I've seen over fifty of them today."

"Are you sure?" said the soldier.

"Yes. I've taught the princess for five years and this isn't her. Princess Cleopatra speaks fluent Greek. It's her mother tongue. I bet this girl won't understand a word."

He switched language, and asked her a question in Greek. Cleopatra looked at him blankly.

"See. Sorry Sergeant, but you are not going to be a hero today. Let her go on her way."

The sergeant nodded. "Well, if you're sure, they can all go."

"You should try colchicum on that boil," said Diodorus. He fiddled around in a satchel and pulled out a small jar.

"Rub this on twice a day, and the swelling will go."

The soldier thanked Diodorus and helped him climb back onto his horse, which had been quietly munching its oats throughout.

Diodorus turned to leave. "I'm afraid I'm getting too old for this sort of caper," he said. "Now what did you say her name was?"

"Mayum."

He leant down to shake Cleopatra's hand.

"Well good luck, Mayum, wherever you are going."

His eyes were twinkling. Cleopatra didn't know why but for some reason her old tutor was letting her go.

21

"**HOW** could you have left without us?" asked Iras once they were safely on deck.

The captain looked shamefaced.

"I saw soldiers doing boat-to-boat searches and whenever they start that you can be held up for hours. I didn't mean to mess you around. Anyway, you're on board now. Here's where you can sleep."

He pointed at the front deck where a broad, white cloth had been stretched from the cabin to the prow to provide shade. The canopy was not high enough to stand under but they could sit comfortably.

In no time they were gliding silently down the canal and out onto the Nile. Cleopatra smiled. Diodorus had set her free. In the space of a day she had swapped a palace for a boat and her clothes had changed from the finest linen to a coarse tunic. She'd left behind her home and her family and yet at least, for now, she was safe. There was nowhere else she would rather be.

Over the next three days she stood for hours at the prow of the boat watching the countryside slide past her. Iras was busy cooking, cleaning and washing while the captain's helper, a wiry boy with a mop of black hair called Nechutes, seemed absorbed in the rigging and sails. Cleopatra tried to make conversation with him at mealtimes but he was only interested in wolfing down his food. He ate as if every meal were his last, never leaving a crumb on his plate, but there wasn't an ounce of fat on him. Iras said he must have known hunger and was anxious to fill up whenever he could.

With nothing much to do, Cleopatra passed the time either helping Iras or watching the farmers at work on either side of the river. In some fields the harvest had begun. Whole villages were working their way through ripe wheat, cutting the stems just below the ears of corn with flint sickles. In the orchards trained baboons picked dates from the tallest trees. Life here was simple and Berenike's coup and her father's escape already seemed like another world. Even the pain of losing Tryphaena seemed to lessen in these peaceful days travelling south.

At night they set up camp round a fire on the riverbank and slept under the stars. The fire kept wild animals away and it was Nechutes's job to make sure that it never went out. Sometimes when the distant howls of lions hunting woke Cleopatra up in the night she would find him looking at her curiously, but he never said a word.

When they moored on the third evening, Iras suggested Cleopatra walk with her to the nearest village to buy food.

"Let's get fresh fish today. I saw some nets close to the boat."

"Oh, I'd love some perch or mullet," said Cleopatra. For three days now they had been eating bean stew.

"Perch?" laughed Iras good-naturedly. "I'm afraid you're going to have to get used to bony old carp. It's all we can afford now."

They went to the water's edge, disturbing a cormorant, which fluttered out of the papyrus reeds. In the shallows six stakes stood in the river bed. Between them someone had hung nets to trap the fish they must have driven towards the banks. Iras looked around her.

"Where is the man?" she said to herself irritably. "You'd think he'd be grateful for the chance of a customer."

"Do you want me to go and look in the village?" asked Cleopatra.

"No, I'll go. You wait here. See if you can pick one that looks good."

Cleopatra looked down at the grey carp. They all seemed the same to her so she decided to choose the plumpest. Maybe it would taste better. But once she'd chosen it she got dizzy trying to track its quick, darting movements through the water. Iras seemed to be taking forever. Although it was evening, the day was still hot, so she sat down in the reeds by the riverbank. As she settled she noticed not ten feet away two unblinking yellow eyes rise from the water. A crocodile. She was sure it was a crocodile. She'd never seen a real one before but she'd heard many stories about them coming out of the river at ferocious speed and carrying off grown men; this one would have no trouble with her.

Oh no, she thought. *What do I do now?*

CLEOPATRA stared at the yellow eyes. Had the crocodile noticed her? She wasn't sure. Should she run or would that make it attack? And what about Iras? She'd be coming back at any moment and would be bound to disturb it. Cleopatra was frozen in terror when, just to her left, she saw Nechutes paddling silently up the river on a small reed vessel. He lifted his finger to his lips, signalling to her to remain still. With relief she realized he must have seen the beast. A moment later he raised his arm and splashed an oar on the river's surface. The animal turned in rage towards the sound and as it turned Nechutes called out, "Run!"

She got up and sprinted, and in her blind haste she bumped straight into Iras.

"There's a crocodile!" she screamed. "Nechutes needs help!"

"Cleopatra, go! I'll get someone."

Iras shouted at some men in a nearby field. From a safe distance, Cleopatra could see the crocodile tugging at Nechutes's paddle. He must be only about her age and he was slightly built. She saw he was struggling to keep hold of the paddle and stay balanced on the reed raft. The crocodile's tail was thrashing around, splashing water high in the air.

Please hold on until those men get to you, she thought. *Oh please hold on.*

The farmers were now in boats and paddling out towards the beast. Some rowed while others beat the water to scare the animal away. At last one of them reached the raft and Nechutes jumped to safety. Sensing defeat, the crocodile dipped below the surface and disappeared.

Iras returned to Cleopatra's side, breathing heavily.

"I should never have left you alone by the river. Normally they don't come this close to a village, but I shouldn't have taken the risk."

"Don't blame yourself," said Cleopatra. "Honestly, I'm fine. Nechutes just saved my life. Wait here."

The boy was standing alone on the riverbank, the men having returned to their work in the field now that the drama was over. Cleopatra approached him slowly. They had hardly exchanged a word in the past three days and she didn't know where to start.

"How can I thank you?" she said. "That was so brave."

"Not really," he answered. "My father was an animal trainer. I grew up with them. You learn their ways."

"But that was a wild crocodile. You risked your life for mine and you don't even know me."

"I do know you." Nechutes looked at the ground as he spoke to avoid her gaze. "The market was full of talk about a missing princess on the day we left. I suspected it was you when I saw you desperately chase after the boat and then I thought I must have been wrong when the soldiers let you go. But just now Iras called you 'Cleopatra', when she was in a panic, so I guess I was right in the first place." His tone was firm but not threatening.

"Cleopatra's my middle name."

"I don't think so," said Nechutes quietly.

"You're wrong..." she faltered, "I'm Iras's daughter. We're going to a wedding in Dendera and then returning to our farm."

Nechutes finally looked up from the ground and met Cleopatra's gaze. "Show me your hands. Let me see your palms."

She turned them over for his inspection.

"Not a callus on them," he laughed gently. "Those hands have never done a day's work in a field."

She could see that it was hopeless trying to convince him otherwise.

"What are you going to do?" she asked simply.

"Why did you run away?" responded Nechutes, not answering her question.

Cleopatra looked around her, making sure that no one was in earshot. She spoke softly. "I thought I'd be killed by the new queen. My eldest sister, Tryphaena, was murdered four days ago. I would have been next, I'm sure of it."

"Oh."

"Are you going to report me? You'd be well rewarded by the palace for it," she added bitterly.

"No. Why would I do that? I won't tell a soul."

He said the words quietly and firmly. It felt like a promise. Cleopatra breathed a sigh of relief.

"Anyway I'm running away too, in a way," he continued. "The captain thinks that I'm an orphan and I suppose I am. After my parents died I was sold to a farmer as a slave. He beat me all the time so I escaped from him after last year's flood and got this job."

Cleopatra understood that by taking her into his confidence Nechutes was showing her that she could trust him.

"Aren't you scared of being recognized as you go up and down the river?" she asked.

"We travel between Alexandria and Syene. My village is south of the first cataract. As long as we don't cross it then I'm safe."

"But the captain said he was travelling to Nubia. That's way further south."

"I know. I'm going to leave before Syene but I'll get other work on the river."

"Why don't you find work on the land, far away from your village?"

"I love this river. It's my home and I could never leave it. You won't tell anyone my plans will you?" It was the first time she had seen him smile.

"Of course not. But if there is ever anything I can do

to repay you then I will do it. I'm not in much of a position now, but if I ever am again you will ask, won't you?"

"I don't want anything from you," said Nechutes. "That's not why I—"

"I know," interrupted Cleopatra. "That's not what I meant."

23

THE days passed uneventfully as they continued on their journey south. Since the incident with the crocodile, Cleopatra and Nechutes had become friends and Nechutes was no longer the shy boy who seemed to be always at the opposite end of the boat from her.

The strip of green, fertile land on either side of the river narrowed once they passed the pyramids at Memphis, until the desert was visible on both sides, sometimes in the distance, at other times only a field away.

At last they came to the great temple of Dendera and Cleopatra knew that her journey was almost over. The captain moored the boat below the temple walls to allow Iras to get some last provisions while he made arrangements with a merchant for a future trip. Iras warned Cleopatra to stay on board. Pilgrims travelled from all over Egypt to Dendera and someone from Alexandria might be in town and recognize her.

Cleopatra sat on the deck, frustrated at being so close to the famous temple and yet unable to see it. Nechutes came over carrying a small bundle.

"Mayum, I'm going."

"Already? I thought you were travelling as far as

Thebes," she said.

"With both of them gone I've got a good chance to escape now, before I get too close to home. I might not get another."

"What are you going to do?"

"I'll find a boat that's heading north," said Nechutes. "There are plenty of them around."

Even though she had known that they would soon be parted, Cleopatra wasn't ready to say goodbye to her first real friend.

"I wish you weren't going," she said.

"I have to."

"Well, at least let me give you this to remember me by." She took from around her neck a tie with a small leather box, the size of her little finger, attached to it.

"Look inside."

Nechutes undid the tiny lid and pulled out a little roll of papyrus and a miniature gold scarab beetle.

"It's a certificate from the Temple of Isis promising the wearer divine protection," explained Cleopatra as Nechutes looked uncomprehendingly at the paper. "The beetle will ensure you good health. It's gold so it won't tarnish. It'll keep its power forever. My father gave it to me."

"I can't take these," said Nechutes.

"I want you to have them. You saved me from that crocodile and you've been a good friend. Keep them until we meet again. Anyway," Cleopatra said, "do you think Iras would trust me to one amulet?" She raised her hands and jangled a charm on each wrist.

"Thank you," said Nechutes. "I'll come and visit you when I can."

Iras and the captain returned as the sun was getting low in the sky. The captain waited half an hour before giving up on Nechutes and sailing off without him, commenting only that there were plenty more boys where that one came from.

The next morning Iras woke Cleopatra up early. They packed their small collection of belongings, tied them up in a bundle, and sat on deck ready to leave at the next village. As they got off, the captain was already engaging another boy to help on the boat. Cleopatra thought of Nechutes. He was right; he would get work easily enough.

"Now, Mayum," said Iras, "it's just a short walk to the village you see up there on the hill."

Cleopatra looked ahead. There was Bahri. It was indistinguishable from the hundreds of villages she had seen along the river. But this one was going to be her home.

24

IRAS woke Cleopatra.

"Come on, my little farmhand. You need to get up now."

Cleopatra opened her sleepy eyes and pushed off her itchy goat-wool blanket. Through the high window she could see that the sky was still grey. The sun could hardly be above the horizon.

"Why so early?" she moaned.

"The Nile waters are beginning to rise. We need to get the last of the crops in before the river floods the fields and ruins everything."

Drowsily, Cleopatra stretched. Her body ached. The thought of another day picking up corn and barley heads cut by the men was grim. The soft skin on her palms was blistered and bled and yet she couldn't rest. As Iras said, the crops had to be harvested.

They had now been in Bahri for over a month. Iras's brother, Cheti, had welcomed them into the family home. Iras had told him that she was now a widow and that her husband had been from Cyprus – which accounted not only for Cleopatra's lighter colouring but also for her ability to speak Greek. She'd worked in the palace but fled to Bahri when the king went to Rome.

The new queen didn't trust any of the king's servants and it wasn't safe for her to remain in Alexandria.

Cheti readily accepted Iras's story. He had no reason to doubt his sister, who he hadn't seen for many years, and was glad of the additional help. He was a widower himself and a father to two children, Pepi and Charmian.

"Where are the others?" said Cleopatra, sitting up and noticing that the two sleeping benches opposite were empty.

"They're already working. Cheti got them up before dawn."

Cleopatra groaned. *If it wasn't for Pepi*, Cleopatra thought, *I'd be happy to hide in Bahri until Father returns.* She felt safe; it was impossible for Berenike's soldiers to search every village in the country. She knew that she would get used to the work and she could put up with sleeping on a hard bed surrounded by garlic cloves to ward off snakes. She was even beginning to like bean stew. But she would never, never get used to spending day and night with that horrible boy and his wimpy sister.

"Why did you let me oversleep?" grumbled Cleopatra as she dressed. "You know Pepi will tease me again and say I can't keep up."

"Mayum, you could do with a little rest. You've been working hard. And it's hardly late, the sun isn't up yet. It won't make any difference to your cousins."

"It will to Pepi."

"Well, I think you're doing more than your share," answered Iras. "And you must remember to be grateful that Cheti took us in. What would we have done without him? So for Isis's sake, learn to get on with his son. He'll be going back to school when the flood starts."

That's easy for you to say, thought Cleopatra as she grabbed some bread from a jar by the oven and raced to catch up. She was the one that had to try to control her temper all day in the hot sun while working next to him.

"Which field are they in?" she called as she left.

"The barley meadow, right on the river bank."

Cleopatra headed off at a trot through the village. Bahri consisted of around twenty mud-brick homes clustered together on high, rocky land where the desert met the fertile valley. Below the houses, fields ran down to the river's edge. The land was criss-crossed with canals carrying precious water from the Nile.

The early morning walk was beautiful. A flock of pelicans were honking in the rushes and the air was still. The sun, which was now a semi-circle rising behind the cliffs, turned everything golden. The land looked so peaceful and undisturbed that Cleopatra felt like skipping until she saw Pepi in the distance.

Her cousin was thirteen and tall for his age. Cheti was ambitious for his only son and was sending him to train as a scribe at the temple school in Dendera. Pepi was the first member of his family to learn to read and write; unfortunately he couldn't wait to show off about it. Evening after evening Cleopatra seethed in silence as Pepi, sprawled across the only bench so that she and Charmian had to sit on the floor, boasted about all the things he'd learnt. She longed to shout out loud, "I know that too!" but of course she couldn't. How would Iras ever explain that the daughter of a servant could read and write? And that wasn't the worst of it. Pepi appeared to have taken against Cleopatra from the moment she arrived. He teased her mercilessly for her inability to make bread, cook and wash clothes. Cleopatra wasn't used to being treated this way. She let it rile her when she knew she shouldn't and many an evening Iras had to give her a quiet talk about getting on with Pepi.

Charmian, the younger cousin, was ten years old and quite unlike her brother. He was a tall, strong-looking boy, whereas she was slight. He could be loud and boorish, while she was meek and hardly said a word. The only things they seemed to have in common was straight, jet-black hair and nut-brown skin.

"Nice of you to get out of bed," jeered Pepi as she fell in behind him and started collecting the barley.

"It's not my fault. Iras has only just woken me."

"Well, the Nile's not going to wait for you even if Iras does."

"I'm sure we'll get it done. Look, there's not that much left to harvest."

"Oh, now who's the farmer? Why do you think Cheti

got us up early? Or do you, a girl, know better than him how fast the water will rise?"

Cleopatra clenched her fists until her nails dug into her skin, but managed to keep her temper under control.

"I'm sure it'll be fine," was all she said.

"Yeah, well no thanks to you. You're just another mouth to feed round here, you know. You should pull your weight."

Cleopatra bent down and worked as fast as she could but inside she was furious. Whatever she did was wrong in Pepi's eyes and he seemed to take pleasure in letting her know it. Much to her annoyance, tears of frustration welled up. She couldn't control them and a teardrop rolled off her cheek. Charmian must have seen, for she gently touched Cleopatra's arm and said quietly, "Pepi, I'm sure Mayum is working as hard as she can."

"Are *you* answering me back now as well?" Pepi turned on Charmian.

"No," she answered, "of course not."

"Good."

He turned away but Cleopatra observed gratefully that after Charmian's intervention he did leave her alone.

After a morning of work it was time for a break. Charmian was carrying a water jar.

"Shall we go down to the river?" asked Cleopatra tentatively.

Although she had lived with the family for most of

the harvest season she had hardly spent any time alone with Charmian.

They walked a little way and sat between two papyrus clumps at the water's edge.

"Thanks for standing up for me," said Cleopatra. "It was kind of you but you don't have to. I don't want to get you in trouble."

Charmian looked out across the river. "Don't worry about it," she said quietly. "Pepi's not really that bad. He's just anxious about school. That's why he's difficult at the moment."

"What's he worried about?" asked Cleopatra.

"During the flood season he'll be going to Dendera every day to study with the priests. He'll have to work really hard."

"But he loves it, doesn't he? He's always telling us how well he's doing."

"The school costs a lot of money," said Charmian. "Father's going to have to take on extra work to pay for it and he's already in debt so Pepi feels he has to do well."

"I'm sure he will," said Cleopatra, unsympathetically. "Anyway, I'd love to be studying." Recently she'd been missing her lessons with Diodorus. "Charmian, have you ever thought about going to school?"

"No, of course not!" Charmian looked shocked. "The scholars are training to be scribes. That's a man's job."

"But would you like to go?"

Charmian took her time answering. It was as if the

possibility had never occurred to her before.

"Yes," she responded at last. "Yes, I suppose I would. The Dendera temple walls are covered with hieroglyphs. It would be wonderful to be able to read them."

"I could teach you. I could teach you to speak Greek and to read and write Egyptian," Cleopatra said eagerly.

"You can read?" Charmian looked at her in wonder.

Cleopatra suddenly felt ashamed. She knew she shouldn't be boasting about her education and yet here she was telling Charmian at the first opportunity. Still, she convinced herself, if she could help Charmian it must be a good thing.

"In Alexandria lots of girls study," Cleopatra said. "Iras didn't tell your father in case he disapproved. But when the floods come and we have a little time we could start our own secret school, just you and me."

"I'd like that," Charmian said. "But now we should get back or Pepi will be on at us again."

As they stood up a rowing boat caught Cleopatra's eye. A boy in a white loin cloth was waving wildly as he came downstream towards them.

"Who's that?" asked Charmian.

"Nechutes!" said Cleopatra excitedly. "He's a friend of mine. I wonder what's brought him here."

NECHUTES'S little boat landed between the rushes. As he tied it up, he explained that this was the first time he'd come south since he'd left her. His new employer was trading locally and he had a whole afternoon free.

"I'm so happy to see you!" exclaimed Cleopatra. "But the water's rising and we have to get the last of the harvest in as quickly as we can. We're going to have to work until sunset."

"That's all right," said Nechutes. "I'll help in exchange for a meal."

Iras arranged an early supper so that Nechutes wouldn't be late getting back to his new captain. As the sun set, the family sat round the fire eating a roasted hare that Cheti had caught with a sling.

Nechutes wolfed down his meat. Iras loaded up his plate again and in a moment it was gone. She offered more.

"He's eating like a hog. There'll be nothing left for the rest of us," complained Pepi.

Nechutes blushed and he shook his head awkwardly.

"Thank you, Iras. It was very good, but I'm full," he said quietly.

Cleopatra was furious. How dare Pepi embarrass her friend?

"Pepi, that's rich coming from you. You eat more than Charmian and I put together."

"I do more work than you two."

He flicked a bean at her.

Iras gave Cleopatra a hard stare. Cleopatra seethed – precious Pepi was never told off. Her nurse turned to Nechutes and changed the subject in an effort to calm the atmosphere.

"Have you been to Alexandria since we last saw you?"

"Yes, I was there ten days ago."

"What's the news?"

"In the market all anybody talks about is the Romans. People are still worried about whether they'll invade or not. So far there's no sign they will."

"Did you hear anything about the king?"

"Yes. He's rumoured to be staying with a general called Pompey in Rome," he replied.

"And?" Iras pressed him further. "Any more gossip?"

"I don't know if what I heard is true," answered Nechutes hesitantly, but Iras pressed him again.

"I heard that a Roman called Cato deliberately called the king to him when he was on the toilet with an upset stomach. He wanted to humiliate him, I suppose."

"Oh no," murmured Cleopatra. "Is that really what people are saying?"

"What are you so upset about, Mayum?" jeered Pepi.

"You're only his servant, you know."

"And Queen Berenike?" asked Iras quickly. "Is she popular?"

"It's hard to tell. She held a lavish funeral for Princess Tryphaena a couple of weeks ago. At every corner there were stalls handing out free meat and wine. It was amazing and of course everybody loved it. But then I heard from someone else that the queen was wicked. He said she'd married a foreign prince but then had him strangled three days later because he was too ugly. So who can tell?"

"Well, Mayum," said Iras, "it does sound as if we were right to leave. It's still very unsettled there."

"I'm sure you're right," answered Cleopatra, but the news of her father's humiliation made her miserable. It was agonizing hearing these snippets of news that must already be weeks out of date. But, of course, what Iras said was true. She was certainly safer here in Bahri, far away from the palace. All she could do now was wait until her father came home and pray that his voyage would be successful.

Slowly the Nile waters rose. At first the water lay in puddles over the fields closest to the riverbank and then the puddles grew and joined up, covering the earth. As each field disappeared, the river grew wider and wider. Villages dotted all along the valley began to look like islands in a vast lake. And still the waters rose.

After many days, the Nile reached its highest point. Now that the fields were under water, no farming was possible, and Pepi began school again. Each morning Cleopatra watched enviously as her cousin packed a bag with cakes of ink, reed pens and a sharp knife for trimming sheets of papyrus.

Over supper Cheti often asked Pepi to tell them what he had done at school that day.

"Where are you in the class rankings? How are you doing?" Cheti demanded. "Are you sure you're going to pass with good marks? Do you need to do extra studying this evening? I could always borrow a lamp."

"No, that's not necessary, Father. Please, it's fine," Pepi always answered.

"What about help from Mayum? Iras tells me that she speaks Greek. Would that be useful?" Cheti continued.

"No. Look, I don't want any interference. Just let me get on with it. I certainly don't need help from a girl."

Cleopatra was always relieved that the exchanges between father and son ended this way. The less time she spent with Pepi, the better.

During the flood Charmian and Cleopatra still had chores each morning. They had to spin wool and weave cloth, collect water in heavy pottery jars, help with the laundry and with baking the bread. But in the afternoon, when the sun was at its shimmering highest and the dry heat made Iras sleepy, they were free to do as they pleased.

Cleopatra was determined to start teaching Charmian. It didn't seem fair that only Pepi could study but she also had a more selfish motive. She hadn't tried to read or write for three months and if she didn't practise her letters soon she was worried she might forget them.

At first Charmian needed cajoling. She knew her father would not approve, for it was unheard of for a village girl to read and he was a traditional man.

Gently Cleopatra persevered. She found a shady date palm, away from the houses and the prying eyes of the villagers, and persuaded Charmian to spend a couple of hours each day with her just to see if she enjoyed it. They would tell Cheti later.

"Let's start with writing," said Cleopatra. "There are twenty four signs for sounds."

Cleopatra took up a stick in the ground and drew an owl in the dust. "That stands for the sound 'm'."

Then she drew a snake. "This sign makes the sound 'z' and this," drawing a hand in the earth, "makes the sound 'd'."

Charmian tried drawing the symbols and repeating the sounds they made.

"Now let's try these ... water for 'n', a foot for 'b' and a bowl for 'k'."

Again Charmian practised the signs and sounds.

Each afternoon they drew more and more until Cleopatra was satisfied that Charmian had drawn all twenty-four symbols correctly and that she had learnt to match the right sound to each symbol.

"If you were learning Greek it would be easy now," said Cleopatra. "You have your collection of letters, called an alphabet, and you put them together to make words you can sound out. Writing our language is harder. Some words we make with sounds and some with pictures. Watch this."

She picked up a sharpened reed and drew a bird. "What do you think this means?"

"Bird, I guess," said Charmian.

"You're right. But what about this?" and she drew a similar bird but with a shorter, thicker neck.

"Small bird?" answered Charmian doubtfully.

"No, it means bad. You have to learn to draw the symbol exactly or the meaning changes."

"Oh my goodness," said Charmian. "How many are there?"

"Over six hundred, but you don't need to know them all. We'll start with the most common ones. Don't worry, you'll pick them up."

Each afternoon they sat under their date tree and practised and practised drawing in the earth with sticks and reeds. Cleopatra was surprised at how much she enjoyed teaching Charmian. But still more surprising was how much she enjoyed Charmian's company. Here was somebody who seemed to like her just for herself. It was so much more rewarding than being with the children who had occasionally been brought to visit her palace apartment. Whatever she'd said they'd always agreed with. But Charmian, despite being quiet, had a strength and dignity about her that Cleopatra couldn't help admiring.

Day after day they studied until Charmian had diligently mastered all the simple hieroglyphs and it was time to move on to something more challenging. Cleopatra took up a stick and drew the sign for "boat" in the mud.

Charmian tried to copy it but it was more detailed than any signs she had drawn so far. Each time she tried Cleopatra looked at it and shook her head. "No, that squiggle at the end is not right," she said, or, "The middle isn't round enough. Can you see in my drawing? Yours is too long – it makes it look too like the picture for wind."

Charmian tried again, but Cleopatra still wasn't happy. At last Charmian threw down her stick in frustration.

"I can't see the differences. Your signs are so roughly drawn it's impossible to copy properly. I give up."

"Charmian, don't," said Cleopatra. "You're doing so well."

"I can't learn with mud and sticks. I'll never be able to draw precisely enough."

Cleopatra nodded sympathetically. It was true. Their equipment was not good enough.

"I know it's difficult, but they're all we've got, unless..." She smiledly mischievously, "unless we can get hold of some proper writing materials."

"How are we going to do that?" asked Charmian. "We don't have any money."

"Pepi has them."

"He's not going to give them to us. You've seen the way he looks after his paper and pens. Anyway, I don't want Father to know yet and I know Pepi would tell him."

"We don't need paper; we can find some broken pottery to use. And we don't need pens; we can make them from reeds. It's only the ink," said Cleopatra, thinking out loud.

An idea was forming in her head, but she was going to need Charmian's help.

26

"CHARMIAN, I'm going to take some of Pepi's ink," Cleopatra said.

"How?" answered her cousin.

"When he's working tonight, you must distract him and get him out of the room. I'll creep in and chip a little off his ink cakes. He won't notice. We don't need much."

"Do you think we should?" asked Charmian.

"Why not? Those cakes last for years and you need the ink."

"But isn't that stealing?"

"No," answered Cleopatra firmly, trying to convince herself as much as Charmian. "It's only borrowing, and I promise that when I'm able, I'll repay Pepi ten times what we take."

That evening when he got home from school, Pepi spread out his work on the floor and settled himself in the one shaft of light that came into the room from the high window. He had only just begun his studies when Charmian ran in breathlessly. Without looking up, Pepi said, "Go away, I'm working. You know that you're not allowed to disturb me."

"But Pepi, there's a hippo nesting in the reeds. I think

the men are going to try to move it on. Don't you want to come and look?"

"You know we shouldn't go near," Pepi answered, but his face was alert. He was taking the bait.

Charmian carried on excitedly, "We won't get too close. If we climb the palm tree by the barley field we'll get a good view."

As the girls had calculated, Pepi couldn't resist. Nobody wanted a hippo to make its home near a village, particularly an aggressive, nesting female, so the men would gather in boats and try to drive it away. Most would slip noiselessly into the depths of the water, never to be seen again, but occasionally one would fight back, using its great jaws to smash through the side of a boat.

"I'll come for just a minute," said Pepi, and they were off.

Cleopatra, who had been waiting out of sight, slid silently around the mud wall and into the room. She knew she didn't have long before Charmian would have to admit that she'd been mistaken. She spotted the two tablets of red and black ink lying among several sheets of papyrus and with a knife cut neatly across the top of each cake, taking only a slither less than half a finger wide. The ink circles in her hand were brittle and crumbly. Taking care not to drop even a fragment, she put the black ink into the amulet pouch she wore around her left wrist and the red ink into a pocket. She then rubbed the tablets with a stone so that the edges looked as rough as when she'd found them. Confident Pepi wouldn't notice any difference, she turned to put them back exactly where she'd found them.

As she did so she noticed the script on Pepi's papyrus. It was Greek. She hadn't read or spoken her mother tongue for so long that she lingered a moment to read a paragraph. But as she looked at the first sentence she realized she could make no sense of it. She tried to say it out loud.

"Go to wel the and fecth watr."

She felt panic rising up in her. Had she forgotten how to speak Greek already? She'd heard about children that could speak a language fluently at the age of seven but couldn't remember a single word a year later if they stopped using it. Could this really be happening to her? She quickly tried the next sentence.

"The frmr the sewed crn seeds n feld."

Again she couldn't make head or tail of it. In alarm she flipped over the papyrus and there at the bottom was a Greek script that she immediately understood.

"Pepi, this work is so full of errors I cannot mark it. Do it again. If you do not make progress I will need to speak to your father."

Relief flooded through her. The note must be from his teacher. She hadn't forgotten anything; it was Pepi who was struggling. She looked at another sheet of papyrus that lay on the floor. This one was covered with hieroglyphs, the same ones that she'd been teaching

Charmian. Again Cleopatra could see that the page was littered with mistakes. At the bottom was another comment from a different teacher. It read:

"Pepi, this still is not good enough. You have not yet reached the standard required of a scribe."

A dog barked in the field outside. Quickly she put the papyrus back where she'd found it and slipped out of the room into the courtyard, moments before Pepi returned.

"Did you get it?" Charmian whispered.

"Yes."

"Thank goodness. Pepi was furious with me. All the way back he was ranting about how much work he's got to do tonight. I felt terrible."

"How's he doing at school? Did he tell you?"

"No, he never does."

"What happens if he doesn't pass his scribe exams?" asked Cleopatra.

"The school's expensive. Father's borrowed a lot of money to pay for it. Pepi will finish at the end of Shemu and then he has to get a job otherwise I don't know how Father will repay the loan."

"What if he can't?"

"I dread to think. I suppose we would get thrown off our land and then I don't know how we'd feed ourselves. But why are you worrying? Pepi always tells Father he's doing fine."

Cleopatra nodded. She didn't want to alarm Charmian

but, from what she had seen, if the family was relying on Pepi they were going to be in trouble. And soon.

CLEOPATRA watched Pepi each night when he came back from school. He was often irritable – supper was late, Charmian was disturbing him, his room was too dark. Cheti was so concerned that he gave in to any demand.

Cleopatra knew that Pepi was prickly because he was worried. Sooner or later he was going to have to tell his father how far he was falling behind. She couldn't help feeling a little sorry for him. He was in an impossible position. Should she do something? Not only had she had individual tuition but she'd had lessons all year round, whereas the temple school was closed for weeks at a time when the boys were needed in the fields. But Pepi would never accept help from her. And even if she could convince him to, she had another nagging fear. If her new family knew how educated she was, wouldn't they become suspicious? Cleopatra knew that she'd risked a lot by teaching Charmian. Iras would be horrified if she knew. But Charmian was a friend and someone she could trust whereas Pepi could never be that. So in the end she watched and fretted but said nothing.

As stealthily as the waters had risen, day by day they

now receded. Bulrushes that hadn't been seen for many weeks began to protrude through the water's surface. Each day more and more of the rich, dark earth emerged and so the planting season began.

"It's disgraceful how the temples are behaving this year," Cheti said one lunch time when the family were sharing a bean and rabbit stew.

"Why? What have they done?" asked Iras.

"They're all so corrupt. Things were bad enough under the old king, but now it's got worse."

"What's getting worse, Uncle?" Cleopatra asked casually, not wanting to give away her keen interest. It was not often that Cheti mentioned the king.

"Stealing from us poor farmers. It's a joke. And what's more, two soldiers came into the village today looking for some runaway from Alexandria. They were questioning all the men and stopping us from working."

Iras and Cleopatra pricked up their ears but Cheti was onto another topic.

"I should have told them that if they were looking for criminals they could start at the temple. Every year we pay our taxes and with that money the king is supposed to repair the canals. It was badly done under Ptolemy but it's much worse now. The priests won't pay for digging out the canal by Melet's field but three more downstream will be useless next year if we don't."

"Why won't the priests give the instructions, Father?" asked Pepi.

"I told you. Greed. They're keeping the money for themselves and the queen's not interested in peasants like us."

"What sort of runaway were the soldiers looking for?" interrupted Iras. Cleopatra knew they were both thinking the same thing. Was the net tightening around them again?

"Some girl. Have you ever heard of anything so ridiculous? How could a child be that important?"

"And what did the men say, Uncle?" asked Cleopatra, as casually as she could.

"Nothing. There's nobody new round here, except you two and we know where you've come from."

"So nobody mentioned us?" persisted Cleopatra.

"Mayum, you're only asking all these questions to avoid working again," taunted Pepi.

"No, I'm not."

"Pepi's right. We should all get back now," said Cheti.

Cleopatra knew it was dangerous to press any more. It might set Cheti wondering.

"Come here, Mayum," said Iras as the others got to their feet.

"What are we going to do?" she said as they'd left.

"Is there anywhere else we could go?" asked Cleopatra. "We can't go back to Alexandria."

"Alexandria, no," said Iras. "I suppose we could head south. Oh, I don't know what's for the best."

"Iras, the soldiers have searched this village. Surely if

they had heard anything they would have come to get us by now. It must be most sensible to stay."

Iras took Cleopatra in her arms and gave her a brief hug. "I hope you're right."

FOR several days Iras was so jumpy she hardly let Cleopatra out of her sight. But as each day passed she relaxed a little more. The soldiers must have been given no useful information and moved on to the next village.

Now that the ploughing was done, Cleopatra and Charmian spent many days sowing seeds and then driving the village cattle across the fields to trample the precious grain into the earth and stop it being eaten by birds.

It was not long before green shoots appeared. The land was so fertile, the barley and wheat seemed to grow before their eyes.

Pepi was now spending more and more time on his studies. At the end of Shemu, the harvest, he was required to hand in compositions in both Greek and Egyptian for his final examination. He had to pass. Cheti was looking more and more anxious and the whole family knew that money was tight. Looking around at the tall fields of crops, Cleopatra calculated that Pepi's deadline must be less than a month away. She tried to reassure herself that he had time to catch up.

She and Charmian now had less time for their "school" than during the flood but they practised when they could. Cleopatra began to teach Charmian to speak Greek. She had heard some words in the market place and made rapid progress.

"Mayum, how do you know so much?" she asked Cleopatra one afternoon as they weeded between the tall ears in a barley field.

"I grew up in Alexandria. It was easy. Everyone speaks Greek there." She longed to take Charmian into her confidence and let her know that the odd thing was not that she spoke Greek, but that she spoke Egyptian. Here, finally, she had a friend and yet she still couldn't be honest.

"I don't mean just the Greek," Charmian persisted. "You can read and write hieroglyphs too. Iras can't do any of those things. Who taught you?"

"I told you, I went to school like Pepi."

"But do all servant children go to school in Alexandria? Even girls?"

Charmian looked so earnest that Cleopatra didn't want to lie.

"No, not all," she answered evasively. The conversation was taking an awkward turn.

"Well, why did you then?"

"It was something my father wanted," she answered, bending over to pull out a stubborn plant with long roots that kept breaking as she tugged at them. "Pass me the spade. I'm going to have to dig this one out."

But Charmian was not to be deflected so easily.

"Were there other girls in your class?" she asked.

"Um…" stumbled Cleopatra, wondering how she could answer truthfully. Just then she spotted a diversion. "Oh look, down there on the river," she cried excitedly. "Can you see the boat? Nechutes is here again. Let's go and meet him."

Together they carried their tools over to the edge of the field, so that they would not be lost in the tall barley, and hurried to the river's edge.

Nechutes trimmed his sail and turned in towards a muddy cove. As the small boat ran aground he leapt neatly ashore and pulled the shallow craft up and out of the water. He set off to find Cleopatra but he hadn't gone ten yards when Pepi stepped out from behind a clump of reeds and blocked his path.

"I see the river rat is back again."

"I'm here to see Mayum. Please get out of my way," answered Nechutes, determined not to be provoked.

"Really? Or just using her to beg another meal?" He flicked the boy's chin with a spiky reed.

"Get lost, Pepi."

"No, you get lost. This is my village, not yours." And with this Pepi put his hands on Nechutes's chest and began to push him back towards the river.

He was a year older than Nechutes and several inches taller. Although Nechutes shoved back, Pepi's greater weight and height gave him an advantage. Nechutes pushed harder, trying to maintain his ground. In the tussle they both lost their balance, tripped over and fell in the mud, wrestling.

"Stay away!" shouted Pepi. "We don't want stinking beggar boys around here."

"It's not your land. I don't need your permission to visit," retorted Nechutes.

As the boys fought Pepi grabbed wildly at a cord tied around Nechutes's neck. The string broke and a small leather box fell to the ground and rolled away.

Both boys got to their feet and raced to pick it up but Pepi got there first. He grabbed the box and held it high out of reach before Nechutes could stop him.

"Give that back!" shouted Nechutes.

"No," said Pepi and slowly, tauntingly, he shook the box open. Into his hand fell the gold scarab beetle that Cleopatra had given Nechutes many months before.

"Not only are you a beggar," Pepi said, staring contemptuously at him, "but you're also a thief."

"No I'm not," protested Nechutes.

"Well how else could you afford this? It looks like real gold."

"It was given to me."

"Yeah, by who?"

Nechutes stayed quiet. He couldn't tell Pepi, for how could Mayum admit to owning such a treasure?

"Well?" said Pepi triumphantly.

Just at this moment Cleopatra and Charmian walked

into the clearing. Cleopatra saw the amulet in Pepi's hand and was furious. Her father had given it to her. How dare Pepi behave so disrespectfully? Never mind what Iras thought, she had had enough.

29

"PEPI, give that amulet back," Cleopatra ordered. "Nechutes is telling the truth. It was a gift. I gave it to him."

Neither Pepi nor Nechutes had heard the girls approaching. They spun round to see Cleopatra standing with her hands on her hips, and a look of fury on her face. Charmian stood two paces behind her.

"You? Yeah right," answered Pepi. "I'm sure you've got lots of gold to dish out. And anyway, who are you to order me about? Get back to the field."

Cleopatra was now so cross that she could feel the blood pounding in her head. Whatever it took she was going to get that amulet back and keep Nechutes out of trouble. Throwing caution to the wind she said, "If you don't give it back, I'll go and tell your father about your school marks."

"What are you talking about?" said Pepi, but with much less confidence than before.

"I've seen your teachers' comments – 'not meeting the standard', 'will have to talk to your father', that sort of thing. Do you want me to go to Uncle Cheti?"

"You wouldn't dare," he said, but she could see the doubt in his eyes.

"Try me."

Pepi clenched his fist in frustration, threw the amulet on the ground and stalked off. But Cleopatra's elation was short-lived, for Charmian and Nechutes were looking at her in bewilderment.

"How did you do that?" they asked in unison.

Cleopatra knew she had some explaining to do. Quickly she told them how she'd come to see Pepi's school work. "There's no way he can write an adequate composition in the month he has left," she finished.

"Why didn't you tell me earlier?" asked Charmian.

"I didn't want to worry you. I'm sorry, I just didn't know what to do."

"But I thought we were friends. Friends don't keep secrets from each other."

"I said I'm sorry," answered Cleopatra. She longed to promise that she wouldn't do it again, but how could she? She was still hiding the greatest secret of all and dreaded to think how Charmian would feel if she ever found out.

"Well, we've got to do something," Charmian said. "I heard Father talking to Iras last night. There's hardly any money left and if Pepi doesn't start working soon, we're all sunk. Mayum, you could help him, couldn't you? Like you have with my lessons. We're going into Dendera tonight to celebrate the festival and I'll try to persuade him then. I am his sister. Perhaps he'll listen to me."

"Are we all going?" asked Cleopatra.

So far Iras had not allowed her to go into the town so

she had missed the festivities the previous year.

"Yes. Iras tried to say that you should both stay at home but Father insisted. It's an important occasion. If the whole household doesn't go, the gods might be annoyed and bring us bad luck."

"How about you, Nechutes?" asked Cleopatra.

"I'm staying overnight. My captain wants to join in the fun."

"Let's meet later then, by the south-west corner of the temple," said Charmian. "It's the one furthest from the entrance, at the back by the sacred lake."

"Good idea," said Cleopatra. "Now you'd better try to calm your brother down. I only seem to make things worse."

THE Festival of Joyous Union was the highlight of the year in Dendera. The statue of the Goddess Hathor was taken out of her temple and presented to the crowds to celebrate the harvest. It then travelled south to Edfu on a glittering barge, a journey of over a hundred miles, and people from every village along the route lined the river and cheered the goddess on her way.

There's no need for Iras to worry about me being recognized, thought Cleopatra as she changed her muddy clothes for a clean tunic for the festival. With each season she became less and less like the princess who had slipped out of Alexandria. She was taller, her skin was a deep brown, her hands and feet were like leather and her clothes were worn. Apart from her precious amulets, hidden in leather pouches, she was indistinguishable from every other peasant girl in Bahri. Even her father, wherever he was, might have trouble recognizing her now.

Dendera was teeming with people in carnival mood. The town was infused with the smell of incense and fresh flowers decorated every building. Priests from the temple were handing out loaves of bread, jugs of wine and slabs of beef cut from whole oxen roasting on spits.

Cheti led the way through the happy crowd. He'd arranged to visit a friend's house where they would have an excellent view of the parade. They stopped halfway and got some food. It was not often that the family ate red meat and Cleopatra enjoyed every mouthful after months of barley soup, beans and game, but she noticed that Pepi hardly ate.

After eating, they jostled their way through the overflowing streets and arrived at a house close to the temple. They exchanged greetings with their host and were then ushered up to a large, flat, mud roof from which they would have a splendid view. Below, hundreds of men, women and children were lining the streets.

To the left of their roof, only a hundred yards away, stood the pylon, the great sandstone wall enclosing the temple. As the sun set, above the noisy street chatter came the sound of a horn and the two great wooden gates in the middle of the pylon creaked open. The tip of Hathor's golden barge emerged to the sound of hundreds of drums. The beat vibrated through Cleopatra, making her body hum. "Come on, Charmian," she said, "let's get as close to the front as we can."

"What about Pepi?" whispered her cousin. "He looks so worried."

"Well, you can't talk to him with Uncle Cheti around," said Cleopatra. "We might as well enjoy the parade and speak to him later."

Finally the last musician disappeared into the distance and the parade was over. Cleopatra had loved every moment of it. The colour, drama and excitement reminded her of Alexandria.

Just then Cheti called out, "Off you go, children. We adults want some time to ourselves."

"I think Cleopatra should stay with me," said Iras.

"Don't be silly," said Cheti. "Let her have some fun. She's old enough."

Thank goodness for Cheti, thought Cleopatra. At last she would get a chance to have a proper look around the town.

"Stay together," shouted Cheti as they left. "Pepi, look after Mayum and your sister."

As soon as they were down on the street, Pepi turned to follow Hathor's barge, which was going in the opposite direction to the temple where they had agreed to meet Nechutes.

"Pepi," said Cleopatra, "Charmian and I promised to meet Nechutes by the lake."

"Forget it. It's bad enough having to look after you but I'm not trailing after you as well."

"We made a promise," said Cleopatra as reasonably as she could. "We can't just leave him there."

"No..."

"Hold on, Pepi," said Charmian, "if you take us to Nechutes then he can look after us for the evening and you'll be free. How about that? I'm sure Father wouldn't mind and anyway he isn't going to know, is he?"

Getting rid of the girl who had humiliated him suited Pepi down to the ground.

"Fine," he said, "but I'm warning you, if he isn't there then you'll have to go where I say."

At the pylon gates they turned left and followed the great wall that encircled the temple and dominated the town. Its stone facade was decorated with carvings of pharaohs, queens and scenes from the life of Hathor. It was also covered with hieroglyphs.

Pepi wove a way through the crowded street with Cleopatra and Charmian following behind. When they were halfway along the eastern wall, to Cleopatra's amazement, Charmian suddenly called out, "Oh look, Mayum, I can read that. It says 'Here lives Hathor, mother of Horus'."

"Don't be stupid. You can't read," Pepi called over his shoulder.

"Look at it," challenged Charmian. "Isn't that what it says?"

Pepi's lips moved silently as he decoded the writing.

"That's a pretty good guess, I suppose. It's not hard though is it," he added sarcastically. "We *are* standing outside the Hathor temple."

"I didn't guess," said Charmian.

"Really? So what does this say?" Pepi pointed to another part of the wall.

Cleopatra stood, transfixed, as her cousin concentrated on deciphering the script. What was Charmian playing at? She said she didn't want her family to know that she could read and write and yet here she was giving the game away.

Charmian paused as her eyes ran up and down the text several times and then she said, "Goddess Nut gives birth to the sun at dawn and swallows it at dusk."

Pepi looked dumbfounded. He had struggled with the hieroglyphs and yet here was his younger sister, who'd never been to school, reading them.

"How did you do that?"

"Mayum taught me."

"What?" he said in disbelief.

"Mayum has taught me to read and write. She's also been teaching me to speak Greek."

Pepi looked at Cleopatra and then at Charmian. He seemed completely bewildered. Finally he said slowly, "You taught Charmian to read?"

"Yes," Cleopatra answered, still confused.

"And she can help you too, Pepi," interrupted Charmian quickly. "I know you need help with your examinations. We're relying on you, Father, Iras and I, and if you don't pass we could all starve. Why don't you let Mayum help? You can see what a good teacher she is."

Now Cleopatra understood what Charmian was trying to do. It was a good idea, but doomed of course. Pepi would hate her more than ever.

Just then a trumpet blew loudly, away to their left, drowning out any response Pepi might have made. After several blasts they heard the stamp of many feet. The ceremony at the river must have finished and the priests were returning. All along the road people backed out of the way and fell to their knees.

"Make way! Make way!" called out a young man, emerging from a side street. He was carrying a flaming torch high in the air which made his bald head shine in the evening light. Twenty feet behind him came a cohort of men dressed in the white robes and papyrus sandals of the temple and marching in a rectangular formation. In the centre of this protective ring was a tall, thin priest in a leopard-skin cape and a jewel-encrusted collar. Around his wrists were gold bangles but his arms were so scrawny that they hung absurdly loose. Cleopatra looked at him curiously. He had penetrating eyes painted with dark kohl. Suddenly a chill went down her spine. It was Pshereni, Berenike's priest. He must have come to Dendera for the famous festivities. Iras had been right to be worried. She should have taken more care.

Cleopatra shrank back against the wall, praying to Isis to make them turn along the street she had just walked down, but they didn't. As if in slow motion they kept marching straight towards her. Instinctively she backed further away feeling for the wall, but it wasn't stone that her fingers touched. It was wood. In the evening light she hadn't noticed the side door that led into the temple and now here she was, leaning on it and blocking Pshereni's path. There was no way he could miss her.

CLEOPATRA was the only person still on her feet other than the priests. She felt a tug on her little finger – Charmian, who was on her knees, was pulling her down. Quickly she came to her senses and sank to the ground.

Two feet in papyrus sandals stopped in front of her.

"Who are you to block my path?" roared a familiar voice in Greek. Cleopatra now had her wits about her sufficiently not to respond in her native tongue. *Keep playing the innocent peasant*, she said to herself. That was her only chance. It had worked once before. She must be able to do it now.

"I'm sorry, my lord," she murmured in Egyptian.

She heard her response being translated.

"Look at me when you speak," shouted the Greek voice.

Again, carefully waiting for the translation, Cleopatra raised her head and looked directly into Pshereni's cold eyes. His large nostrils were quivering with rage.

Please don't recognize me, please don't recognize me, she prayed silently, again and again.

"I'm sorry, my lord," she said as humbly as she could. "I was confused. I've never been to this town before."

Pshereni looked her over slowly. Then she heard him say to the translator, "Ask her where she's from." Cleopatra's mind raced. She mustn't say anything that could help him track her down if he ever found out who she was.

"Thebes," she answered, praying that neither Pepi nor Charmian would correct her. They must be wondering whether she'd gone mad.

"Ask her why she's in Dendera," barked Pshereni.

"I came with my family to worship Hathor."

He paused again.

"And her name?"

"Puyan." Again she prayed that Pepi would not interfere. She glanced at him. He was looking scared. Hopefully too scared to speak.

Pshereni was still looking straight at her. She tried not to flinch.

"Well, Puyan, if I ever set eyes on you again, you won't get back to Thebes. Do you understand me?"

Cleopatra waited again for the translator and then bowed her head.

The priests resumed their march and passed through the small door, slamming it behind them. Order returned slowly to the street. People pulled themselves up off their knees and got on with their business. As Cleopatra got up, an old man muttered, "You were lucky then, miss. He's a hard man. I've seen that priest send people into slavery for less."

Pepi grimaced at the man and then put his hand tightly round Cleopatra's arm. With the other hand he grabbed Charmian. He marched them in silence up the road and round the corner to the sacred lake. This part of the town was far away from the procession and seemed deserted. Nechutes had not yet arrived.

Pepi checked that no one was within earshot.

"What were you playing at back there, Mayum? You could have had us all killed," he hissed.

"I'm sorry, Pepi, I really am, but I couldn't answer him truthfully."

"Why not? What if he'd demanded to see your family? Didn't you think about that? Father wasn't going to call you Puyan and he wasn't going to say we lived in Thebes. Are you mad?"

"No, but I couldn't risk him coming to try and find me later," she answered.

"Why would he want to come and find you?" asked Charmian, looking bewildered.

"He wouldn't, unless he thought she'd lied to him," interrupted Pepi. "Just you wait until I tell Father."

"Hold on Pepi," said Charmian. "Mayum, do you know that priest?"

Cleopatra felt trapped.

"Yes, I knew him when I was in Alexandria. Before I came to Bahri."

"Who is he?"

"He's called Pshereni."

"So," continued Charmian slowly, piecing things together in her mind, "why didn't he recognize you, if you knew him?"

"I look different now. It's been a long time."

"And why didn't you answer him in Greek?"

"I told you, I didn't want him to remember me."

"Why not? Are you and Iras in trouble? Is that why you came south?"

"Yes, she's in trouble all right," interjected Pepi again. "She's in it up to here."

Suddenly he grinned as if everything had just fallen into place.

"You're a thief, aren't you? That explains where Nechutes's amulet came from. You stole it and now you're in hiding."

"That's not true, is it?" Charmian asked, looking directly at Cleopatra.

"What do you think?" she answered. She needed to know Charmian had faith in her.

"I'm sure it's not, but you've got to tell us what's going on otherwise how can we help?"

"I know what's going on. She's a thief. She hasn't even denied it," said Pepi.

Nechutes stepped out of the shadows. He must have heard the last couple of sentences for he said, "No, that's not it. Mayum, I think you're going to have to tell them who you are and trust them, as you did me."

She nodded. There was no other way out. She was

sure that she could rely on Charmian, but Pepi? She took a deep breath and said quietly, "I'm Princess Cleopatra, the princess that disappeared from Alexandria. Pshereni is one of the people who would love to find me."

There was a moment of silence, broken by Pepi.

"Yeah, and I'm King Tutankhamun."

Charmian ignored her brother. "Are you really a princess?"

"Yes, and Iras is my nursemaid. She brought me to Bahri to protect me when my father, the king, left for Rome."

"Why did you need protecting?"

"Berenike, the queen, killed my older sister, Tryphaena. I thought I might be next."

"So that's why you're so educated. I thought there was something special about you but..."

"For the gods' sake. You don't believe her, do you, Charmian?" said Pepi, rolling his eyes.

"Just think for a moment. Iras worked in the palace for fifteen years. Mayum appears from nowhere. What do we know about Iras's husband? Nothing. And Mayum can read and write better than any scholar in your school and she speaks Greek fluently. I bet you speak other languages, don't you?"

"Yes. Nubian, Hebrew and a little Latin."

Pepi was still looking doubtful.

"You're all mad," he said.

"Pepi," Nechutes said gently, "I've known since I

brought Cleopatra down the river. I heard Iras use her real name once, but it only confirmed my suspicions. The princess has become better at covering her tracks since then."

"I still don't believe it," Pepi said stubbornly.

"Look at these then." Cleopatra untied two thongs from her ankle and wrist and gave the amulets to Pepi. "Read them. They're carved with my true name."

Pepi moved out of the shadows of the temple walls to where he could see more clearly. He turned each amulet over slowly.

"You could have stolen them from the princess when you were in the palace," he said uncertainly.

"Both of them?"

"It's possible," he answered but they could all see that bit by bit he was beginning to believe her.

Cleopatra turned to Charmian. She desperately wanted to explain why she hadn't been honest with her.

"I'm sorry I didn't tell you. There were times when I was tempted, but I promised Iras I wouldn't. It was safest that way. Pepi, Charmian, can I trust you not to tell anybody? My life is in your hands."

"You don't want Father to know?" asked Pepi.

"No, as I said, the fewer people that know the better. Pepi, I'm sorry I threatened you this afternoon. I shouldn't have done that."

There was a long pause and then Pepi said, "Forget it. And don't worry, I won't say a word."

"Thank you, but Pepi, do let me help you with your work."

"Since you're a princess and not just a girl, I'd be honoured," he answered with a grin.

"Never mind that," said Charmian. "Mayum's got other things to worry about now. Do you think Pshereni will remember you later?"

Cleopatra was relieved that Charmian didn't seem to be holding her secret against her.

"Even if he does, he won't know where to look."

"Have you anywhere else to go, just in case?" asked Charmian.

"No, not until my father returns. Nechutes, is there any news from Alexandria?"

Nechutes shook his head.

"No, sorry, I haven't been as far as the coast for a while. But on my way into Dendera I did hear that a travelling wise man from the Museion has set up a tent beyond the sacred lake. I'm sure he'll have news from the north."

"I used to study at the Museion. Did you catch his name?" asked Cleopatra.

"Yes, it was a Greek name... Diodorus, I think."

CLEOPATRA and Charmian entered the large, crowded tent and slipped into the back row. Pepi and Nechutes were outside keeping watch for any sign of Pshereni or his men. Inside, there must have been over a hundred people sitting cross-legged on reed mats listening to news from upriver. Diodorus was standing in the centre. He was as good a public speaker as he was a teacher and everyone was captivated.

At last the talk was over and the crowd began to disperse. Cleopatra lingered with Charmian by one of the tent poles.

"I'm afraid you will have to move, young ladies, we've got to take that stake down," called out the familiar, courteous voice.

Only Diodorus, thought Cleopatra, *would call two peasant girls "young ladies"*.

"Excuse me," he said again, as he walked over, "please could you step aside, otherwise you'll get caught in the cloth." He pointed to the cotton roof.

"Diodorus," whispered Cleopatra in Greek, "don't you know me?"

He looked hard at her, and his old face lit up like a child's.

"Well, well, well. I've been touring up and down the Nile, hoping to see you all these months, and finally it's happened."

"Why did you help me in Alexandria? Why did you let me go?" Cleopatra asked. She had waited so long for the answer.

He glanced around, checking no one was in earshot.

"I was Berenike's tutor and I'm sorry to say but in all my years of teaching I never had a more dangerous student. She was the last person this country needed as queen. I knew the consequences of returning you to her. Princess, you are different. A great future awaits you."

"But what if you had been caught? It could have happened so easily…"

"When I saw you by the river I was certain the gods wanted me to preserve you. Why else were you delivered to me rather than one of Berenike's devoted followers? It had to be worth the very small risk I took. Are you with Iras's family?"

Cleopatra nodded.

"I didn't know the village or I would have come sooner. I tried to find Apollodorus but he's vanished. He's not here with you, is he?"

"No. I haven't seen him since the day we left."

"You must excuse my manners. Who's this you have with you?" he asked, moving effortlessly to Egyptian.

"Charmian, Iras's niece."

"I'm pleased to meet you."

"I need to talk to you," said Cleopatra.

"Yes, of course. Let me help put the tent away and then we can sit by that fire over there. Do you see it?"

He pointed to an area beyond the lake where he had set up camp for the night.

Ten minutes later Cleopatra and Diodorus were catching up on the past year. They spoke in Egyptian so that Nechutes, Charmian and Pepi, who were listening in wonder, could follow the conversation.

Finally they turned to the future.

"Is there any news of my father?"

"Yes. At first the Romans watched to see how Berenike would manage the country but now they seem to be tiring of her. Not because she's wicked, I'm sorry to say. They are more self-interested than that. It's because Egypt is in a shambles. The queen has allowed the priests to become dishonest. There is corruption everywhere and it's bound to disrupt next year's harvest."

"I've seen that for myself. But do the Romans really care?"

"Yes, they need Egypt's grain to feed their soldiers. But the chaos does create a chance for your father."

"They'll help him get back his throne?"

"Maybe."

"Why would they be willing to do that rather than conquer us like they have so many other countries? Then they could have all the wheat they wanted."

"Their empire is stretched and they do not have the

soldiers to spare. A king that will do their bidding will keep them happy, at least for a while. Also there is a rumour that your father has promised them ten thousand pieces of silver if they restore him to the throne."

"But that's more than the treasury receives in a year. How ever will he afford it?"

"By raising taxes."

"Farmers can't afford to pay any more," said Cleopatra indignantly. "I've seen how little they're allowed to keep as it is."

"Then I see you haven't been wasting your time here," smiled Diodorus.

Cleopatra shrugged her shoulders. Maybe her teacher was right. By living and working in Bahri she had learnt valuable lessons that would have been impossible to learn in the palace. If she ever got back to Alexandria she promised herself she would use them wisely.

"If Father does return, how do you think he will be welcomed?" she asked.

"You know that the king was not held in – how can I put this – the highest esteem. But Berenike is hated. I think the people will prefer anyone to her, and they would certainly prefer Ptolemy to a Roman occupation."

Cleopatra nodded.

"So is it safe for me to come home yet?"

"No, certainly not." The old man shook his head emphatically. "The Romans will come with the warmer weather. Until then, Princess, you must stay out of sight. Alexandria is even more unsettled than when you left. Berenike is bickering with Achillas and Pshereni. The palace has no money to pay even its own soldiers. There'll be more riots and you don't want to get caught up in all that. You must be patient. I promise I'll send for you when the time is right. Until then, can I trust these young friends of yours to protect their future queen?"

Pepi, Charmian and Nechutes nodded fervently.

"Queen?" said Cleopatra.

"I think that is what the future might hold. When your father returns Berenike will pay heavily for her disloyalty. The princes are still young. You, Cleopatra, are next in line to the throne."

33

AFTER the excitement of seeing Diodorus it was hard for Cleopatra to settle back into village life. The sun rose and fell, day after day, with little news from Alexandria. Another harvest was collected, her third. She began to feel she would spend the rest of her life marooned in the countryside. Downriver, exciting things must be happening but in Bahri nothing changed. Diodorus had said she might be queen one day but shouldn't a future queen do more than just hide? Cleopatra thought about the promise she had made to Tryphaena. Stay loyal to your father. Iras said being alive was enough but it didn't feel like it.

Her only consolation was that Pepi had graciously accepted help with his work. Cheti agreed to Cleopatra teaching his son if that was what Pepi wanted. He even allowed Charmian to join them. By day they worked their way rigorously through hieroglyphs and grammar. In the evenings, when the fire had died down and the oil in the lamp was exhausted, they lay on their benches practising Greek.

At last the time came for Pepi to write his essays. He banned Cleopatra from looking at his work until the first draft was completed. There was no point, he said, in handing in something that he hadn't done. He needed to reach the required standard himself.

Pepi worked alone in the shadows of an olive tree that grew close to the house. As the girls went about their chores they could see him, deep in thought, sucking the end of his reed brush, with a small pile of the papyrus paper building beside him. On the third day he called Cleopatra.

"Now you can read it and tell me what you think."

Cleopatra took the compositions. Both the Greek and the Egyptian scripts were virtually error free. All their hard work had paid off; Pepi passed the exam easily and got a well-paid job at the temple. Now he was happy and Cheti would be able to pay off his debts.

The weather turned cooler again and still there was no message from Diodorus. Even Nechutes hadn't been seen for weeks. Cleopatra was frustrated. How much longer must she wait?

"Right, you two," called Iras one morning. "Stop moping. I'm going to Dendera to talk to the butcher about slaughtering the pig and I'll have to stay overnight and come back tomorrow lunchtime. Mayum, you can make the bread and Charmian, prepare the bean stew."

Cleopatra took several handfuls of grain and began crushing them in the limestone mortar while Charmian sat next to her cutting up onions. They had only just started when a little brown skylark fluttered down and landed on Cleopatra's shoulder. It dropped a nut from its tiny beak. Cleopatra smiled and looked around.

"Nechutes, I know you're there," she called out.

"Is there any news?" she asked eagerly as soon as Nechutes stepped out from behind the tree trunk where he had been hiding. She was desperate to hear what was happening in the North.

"Yes, your father's set sail from Rome. He should be landing in Alexandria in a couple of weeks."

"Really?" Suddenly she felt alive. "So does Diodorus say I should come back?"

"Not yet," said Nechutes. "He wants you to wait until the Roman army has defeated Berenike, but it can't be long now."

Cleopatra felt deflated.

"How long are you here for?" she asked. "When's your captain sailing?"

"I don't have one. I've got my own boat now," said Nechutes proudly.

"How did you manage that?" asked Charmian.

"Diodorus and I have become friends. He comes down to the lake to get news of you when he can. One day he offered to lend me money to buy a boat and since then I've been working every day the gods send to pay him back. That's why I haven't been able to stop. And now it's almost done. I've got a job sailing north tomorrow from Dendera to Alexandria and after that I'll be able to make the final repayment. Then I can spend my life on the river as my own boss. It's what I've always wanted."

"Congratulations, Nechutes," said Charmian. "You must be very pleased."

Nechutes grinned.

"I am. I've got to go and load the boat but I wanted to let you know about your father as soon as I could."

Cleopatra didn't know what to think. It was the news she had been waiting for. But her father was coming home and she wouldn't be there. Iras and Diodorus were so cautious they would keep her safely in the village forever if she let them. Maybe the time had come to take things into her own hands.

THAT night, when she was sure the household was asleep, Cleopatra crept out of bed and piled her few possessions onto a sheet to tie in a bundle. All day she'd been preoccupied with how to help her father and the more she thought about it the more certain she became of one thing – there was nothing she could do in Bahri. She must go to Alexandria. Iras was away and Nechutes was sailing there early in the morning. She wouldn't get a better chance.

She rummaged around looking for a slip of papyrus and a pen. This was not going to be an easy letter to write. *I owe Iras so much but I have to go*, she thought. *I'm fourteen. I'm not a child any more. I've got to make decisions for myself.* And then there was Charmian. They'd lived in each other's pockets for so long. She would miss her terribly. She would explain as best she could to both of them in the note she was leaving.

"Mayum, what are you doing?" Charmian turned over and rubbed her eyes. The scratching of the reed pen must have woken her up.

"Nothing. Go back to sleep."

Instead Charmian sat bolt upright, suddenly wide awake.

"You're leaving, aren't you?"

Cleopatra nodded.

"Why? What about Iras? You've got to tell her."

"Charmian, you know what she's like," sighed Cleopatra. "She won't want me to go home until all Father's enemies are safely behind bars. But I can't do that. I'm a princess and I have to find a way to help my country if I can. I've been thinking about it all afternoon. I'm going to find Nechutes's boat and sail with him."

"Then I'm coming with you," said Charmian resolutely. She jumped out of bed and started pulling on her shabby dress.

"What?" Cleopatra was astonished. It hadn't occurred to her that Charmian might join her. "You can't leave Cheti."

"Pepi's here. He'll be well looked after."

"But I don't know what's going to happen when I get to Alexandria. It'll be dangerous. I can't let you risk your life."

"I want to. What greater honour could there be than to serve a princess of Egypt?"

"Charmian, the honour would be mine," answered Cleopatra honestly. "In the palace it's so hard to have true friends. If you'll promise you'll always be that, then thank you for coming. Now let me finish this note for Iras. Can you get some bread and dates? I don't know how early Nechutes plans to set sail but we can't miss him."

As they drifted along in Nechutes's boat they asked for news at every village. It seemed that an advance party of Romans had landed in Alexandria and Achillas was gathering troops to defend the city. Boats were streaming up the river, taking women and children as far away from the impending battle as possible. Eerily, they were the only ones heading north.

At last they could see the outskirts of the city. Its white stones dazzled on the horizon but there was none of the smoke or flames they'd been expecting. Instead seagulls swooped and squawked in the bright blue sky.

Nechutes moored on the busy quayside. The shore of the lake was crowded with yet more people desperately trying to get away.

"What's going on?" he asked the captain of a nearby boat.

"The Romans are coming. They're at Pelusium. Everyone wants to get out before they arrive."

"Has there been any fighting yet?"

"I don't know any more than what I'm telling you, but who wants to be in a town when soldiers start looting?"

Nechutes reported back to Cleopatra and Charmian.

"Are you sure you don't want me to take you back to Bahri, to wait until things are more settled?" he asked.

"No," said Cleopatra. "I've come too far for that."

"Then I'm coming with you," said Nechutes resolutely.

"No, don't. I don't want you to risk your life as well."

"Mayum, I can't leave you here."

He picked up a small bag.

"Come on."

He pulled off the amulet she had given him and put it in the palm of her hand. "And take this," he added. "You might need it more than me."

Cleopatra smiled.

"Nechutes, I'm grateful. I truly am."

Together the three of them stepped down onto the wet, stone pier at the water's edge. Two and a half long years ago, Cleopatra had left from this very spot, and now she was returning, older, wiser she hoped, but to what?

Twenty minutes later they emerged from the narrow side streets onto the Canopic Way. As usual it was full of people but now they were carrying bundles and pulling carts overflowing with pots and clothes and children. Less than ten miles away a battle was raging between Berenike's men and the king. It wouldn't be long before the victor would enter the city.

"What shall we do now?" asked Charmian.

"We're going there." Cleopatra pointed at the great stone walls that surrounded the royal palace.

"How will we get in?" asked Charmian in dismay. "Won't it be guarded by Berenike's men?"

"Don't worry," answered Cleopatra. "I know a secret way. Nobody will see us. Come on."

CLEOPATRA led Charmian and Nechutes to the palace. She was impatient to be home. The ramparts loomed strong and imposing ahead of them, but they circled round until they came to the far corner where the walls met the coast and Cleopatra stopped beside some thick ivy.

"The door is behind these leaves. The key should be under here," she whispered. "I saw my guard bury it when I ran away with Iras. He promised it would be here when I returned."

She looked left and right, checking that nobody was about and then knelt down, lifted a small boulder and dug quickly into the sandy earth.

"Here it is," she said, triumphantly holding up an old, iron key, the size of her hand. "It's a little rusty, but it should still work."

She pushed it into the keyhole but the lock was stiff. It needed all her strength before it turned and the door creaked open.

"Inside! Quick!"

In the darkness Cleopatra felt for the point where the doorframe met the floor and counted three bricks across and twelve bricks up. There was the shelf dug into the wall. She groped for the flint and lit the lamp Apollodorus had left by the entrance to the passage and then started walking into the blackness. Charmian and Nechutes followed.

The stone path inclined gently upwards into the heart of the palace. At the end of the passageway Cleopatra extinguished the flames, just as Apollodorus had shown her, listened and then slowly opened the door. Luck was with them. There was no one about. They walked into the main corridor, and turned immediately right in the direction of the royal apartments. Cleopatra wasn't sure what she would find – would Berenike be in the palace or on the battlefield, or would she have already run away? And what of her father? Had he come to reclaim his home?

The palace seemed strangely deserted. Cleopatra peered out from behind a pillar at the doors to her father's old rooms. Soldiers had always stood outside when Ptolemy was king, but now the entrance was unguarded. Thank goodness. It must mean that Berenike had fled.

"Come on," she said happily and they ran and slipped through the door.

"Oh," said Charmian, looking around the glittering room in wonderment, "I can't believe how big it is."

"Is that real gold?" Nechutes pointed at a large plate on a wooden shelf.

"Never mind about that, I think I hear voices," said

Cleopatra. "Quick, let's hide."

They dived behind a thick, linen curtain, just as the door was pushed open.

"Pshereni, this is disastrous. I can't believe Achillas has given in already."

Cleopatra immediately recognized her sister's voice. Berenike was still in the palace – and only feet away from them. It was like a nightmare. They mustn't move a muscle. She looked at the others and put her finger to her lips. Cleopatra could see from their pale faces that they understood the danger.

"I'm afraid, Your Majesty, that the messenger was certain of it. Our men were massively outnumbered by the Romans," whined Pshereni. "Many have already deserted."

"The cowards," hissed Berenike. "I knew I couldn't trust them. Did you see anyone guarding the door? Even my own men have run away."

So that's why the palace is so empty, thought Cleopatra. *Nobody wants to be accused of treachery when the king returns.*

"I need to think," Berenike continued. "Father will be here in less than an hour. We must be ready for him."

Her sister sounded frantic. Cleopatra could hear her pacing up and down the room.

"What do you mean?" asked Pshereni. "He'll be surrounded by troops. You won't be able to get to him."

"I know that, you idiot!" she shouted. "But what kind

of reception do you think he's going to give me, eh? And you and Achillas? We'll have one chance and we've got to use it. The man has a weakness. It's the key…"

"The key? How?" asked Pshereni nervously.

"Without the king the Romans will have to do a deal with me. Arsinoe and the princes are too young, and Cleopatra has disappeared off the face of the earth. They don't have enough troops to govern the whole world so they'd have to come to an arrangement with the only royal left. We have to make sure that's what happens."

"Your Majesty?" Pshereni was clearly perplexed.

"You fool. Can't you see? We need to welcome the king in the one way he won't be able to resist. Come here, I'll show you."

Berenike and Pshereni walked to the far corner of the room. Cleopatra strained to hear what they were saying but they were too far away. She peeked around the curtain and saw Berenike open a chest and take out a glass amphora. She poured something onto a handkerchief, which she then twisted in her fingers and put in her pocket. As she turned around, Cleopatra leant back into the shadows.

"I'll do the talking," Berenike said as she left the room. "We'll give King Ptolemy a welcome that nobody will forget. And tell me as soon as Achillas returns from Pelusium. I've got business with him."

They heard footsteps go to the door.

"No, no, my darling," said Berenike, her voice

cloyingly sweet. "You must stay here."

There was the clank of metal on stone and then the door closed.

Cautiously Cleopatra pulled the curtain back a couple of inches. There on the floor lay an enormous leopard. It had to be Nefer. But Nefer was no longer a fluffy cub, she was a fully grown, wild animal. Around her thick, muscular neck was a diamond-encrusted collar and chain, which was hooked on a catch by the door.

Suddenly, Nefer realized she was not alone in the room. She growled and leapt towards the curtain but her chain was just too short and her great paws slipped on the red, marble floor. Cleopatra jumped back and the leopard snarled in frustration.

"What on earth was that?" asked Charmian and Nechutes.

"A leopard. Berenike's tied it up by the door. Unless we can get past it there is no way out."

36

"WE'RE stuck," said Charmian.

They looked at Nefer. The leopard was now pacing a semicircle, growling and spitting and pulling her chain to its maximum length. Her white teeth looked as sharp as needles and her amber eyes glowed with fury. Trying to get past would be madness.

"At least I can find out what Berenike took from that chest," said Cleopatra.

She crossed the room. The sycamore box that Berenike had been rummaging in only moments before was still open. There was the amphora with a glass stopper in it. Cleopatra examined it carefully. Inside was a fine, white powder. Gingerly, she pulled out the stopper, making sure she didn't spill a grain, and smelt it. Nothing. It was odourless. Next to the box was a plate of figs. She pulled one apart and sprinkled some of the powder onto its pink flesh, taking care not to touch any of the fine dust. It seemed to melt away into the fruit's juices. *It has to be poison*, thought Cleopatra, throwing the fig away carefully. Probably the very same potion was sprinkled on Tryphaena's food. Her sister was going to strike again – they had to stop her.

"Berenike's going to poison the king. I'm sure of it.

We've got to get to him before she does."

"How? We're not going anywhere," said Charmian.

"We must do something," said Cleopatra. "You heard her; he'll be here within the hour."

They all looked at the pacing leopard.

"It's hopeless," said Charmian.

"No it's not," Nechutes said resolutely. "I grew up with animals, remember. I'll distract her so you can get out."

"How?" asked Cleopatra.

"When she gets close, I'll grab her."

"You don't understand," said Cleopatra. "Berenike has trained that leopard to savage anyone who comes near her. Even as a cub she was vicious."

"Give me the poison," said Nechutes.

"How will you get her to eat it? And anyway you don't know how long it will take to work."

"Well, we can't just sit here. You said that yourself. So, when I say run, you must go, and don't come back until you've done what you need to do."

"You're going to get yourself killed," said Cleopatra.

"There are more important things at stake," Nechutes answered. "You know that."

His wiry body was taut with tension, but Cleopatra could see that he was determined. And she knew that he was right. She had to do what she could to warn her father. Reluctantly she gave Nechutes the amphora and took Charmian's hand.

"Get as close to the door as you can," Nechutes said.

The girls did as they were told and Nechutes went to the other side. The leopard was now pacing in a semicircle between them, straining on her leash and growling with frustration. Just as she was turning away from him, Nechutes ran towards her and grabbed her collar.

"Run!" he shouted.

Cleopatra and Charmian ran for the door. Behind them they could hear yowling and a cry of pain from Nechutes.

"We've got to help him," said Charmian as soon as they were outside.

"How?" said Cleopatra. "What can we possibly do? He did it so we can save the king. Don't you see? We mustn't waste a moment of the precious time he's given us – that's what he would have wanted."

"WHERE are we going?" asked Charmian as she hurried after Cleopatra down a wide corridor.

"The throne room. That's where Berenike will receive him. Come on, it's this way."

They turned down one passage after another. To Cleopatra the palace was strangely silent, as if a spell had been cast over it and spirited everyone away. If only the magic would allow her to see what had become of Nechutes. She shook herself – she must forget about him for now and think only of saving her father.

Suddenly they heard the sound of horses' hooves clattering on stone and ran to a small window in the stairwell that looked directly onto the courtyard. It was filling with soldiers and cavalry, all dressed in the scarlet uniform of the Roman army.

"Look, that's my father! Can you see him, riding a black horse?"

Cleopatra pointed to the man dressed in purple at the front of the cavalry. He pulled up his horse and jumped down.

"He'll be with Berenike at any moment, come on!" she said excitedly.

They ran down the last few steps, careful to stay out

of sight. Ahead of them, Roman soldiers were blocking the entrance to the throne room but they could see it was crowded with courtiers. Berenike must have rounded up everyone she could find.

"Look at us," murmured Cleopatra, pulling at her ragged dress. "We look like servants. They're never going to let us in."

"Watch out," warned Charmian. She pointed to a young girl stepping out of a side door opposite them, carrying a tray of food. The girl was waved through into the chamber by the soldiers.

"Why's Berenike ordering a feast now?" asked Charmian as another girl passed by with a bowl piled high with grapes.

"Who knows?" answered Cleopatra.

Another servant girl passed and then another, and each was waved through into the hall. This had to be their way in. With so many girls coming and going, surely two more would go unnoticed. Cleopatra tugged Charmian's arm.

"Let's join them."

"Won't someone spot us?"

"I don't think so. I've been in the palace kitchen before. It's always mayhem just before a feast."

They slipped through the side door, which led directly to the kitchen. The large room was in uproar. Pots were boiling over and fires were blazing; steam and smoke filled the room. Cooks were busily serving up pigeon stew, quails, roast lamb and beef ribs onto gilded plates. As soon as a plate was full it was picked up by the head of a line of servants and carried away.

"Don't let it get cold, you idiot," shouted a sweating chef at a boy struggling with a large dish of stuffed ducks, "or the queen will be after me."

Everybody was far too frantic to notice two new faces. Cleopatra and Charmian joined the queue waiting for food. In no time they were at the front and each lifted a plate of roast lamb and walked out. There wasn't a moment to lose.

The throne room was the grandest room in the palace. Its walls were hung with Indian silks and its floor was of polished alabaster. It was full of couches and divans, all of them occupied by senior courtiers in their finest clothes, facing a platform at the far side of the room. On it stood two chairs inlaid with semi-precious stones. Berenike sat in one with Pshereni standing behind her. There was no sign of the king.

Although the room was crowded, it was strangely quiet, as if all those present were nervously wondering what kind of reception the returning king would give them. Cleopatra felt little sympathy. They had all chosen to follow Berenike.

The servants were spreading out now, putting food on tables. Cleopatra slowly walked towards the furthest corner and set down the lamb. Out of the corner of her eye she saw Charmian do the same. Had they come too soon? She didn't want to leave and have to go back to the kitchen for another round of food in case she missed her father, but she had no choice. She couldn't just stand there.

Quickly she raced back to the kitchen, grabbed a dish of pomegranates and hurried back. He still wasn't there. How long could she keep going without someone in the kitchen asking questions? Another round and now she was carrying honey cakes; Charmian had bowls of olives. As she set the cakes down, a gong sounded. At last the king had arrived. Everyone got to their knees and a hush fell across the room. *Perfect*, thought Cleopatra, *no one will notice if I stay kneeling here.*

38

KING Ptolemy the Twelfth, accompanied by a Roman general, strode through the crowded room and onto the platform.

"Your Majesty," said Berenike in a loud voice that didn't waver, "I have gathered all the courtiers here to welcome you back. As you see, we have prepared a feast in your honour."

Cleopatra was amazed. Did Berenike really think the king would believe her?

Ptolemy smiled coldly.

"Welcome me back?" he said sarcastically. "Berenike do not insult me with this stupidity."

Berenike grabbed his hand.

"I hope the Romans have not tried to poison you against me, your own flesh and blood, when all I ever tried to do was keep the throne safe for you until your return."

The king laughed.

"And what about the welcoming party led by Achillas? Their bows and arrows were not too friendly."

"He's a traitor. I've already had him arrested and hanged. Pshereni, a man of the temple, will give you his word."

Cleopatra was amazed at her sister's cruelty. Achillas had been Berenike's partner in all this. She had seen them plotting together. And now her sister had killed him to save her own neck.

"Berenike," said the king, "you won't make a fool of me."

"Father, at least allow me to toast your return."

She clapped her hands and a young woman appeared carrying a tray with a jug of wine and glasses. Cleopatra recognized her immediately. It was Lysandra, Berenike's longest-serving maid.

Cleopatra's heart was pumping wildly. Berenike knew that her father loved wine more than life itself. Surely that was what she meant when she said she would use his weakness. But she had to be sure. If she accused her sister wrongly she wouldn't get a second chance. She watched intently as Berenike filled two glasses, looking carefully for any sign of the handkerchief she had seen her put the powder in, but there was none.

The king waved his hand.

"I'll not drink with a traitor," he said.

"Perhaps you don't trust the wine," answered Berenike, goading her father, daring him to try it.

Then she turned to Lysandra. "Here, show the king that it is made from the best grapes in Egypt."

The girl nervously took a gulp. Nothing happened.

"It's delicious, Your Majesty," she murmured quietly.

Cleopatra watched her father. He knew how long

Lysandra had served Berenike. She had looked after her since she was a child, just as Iras had cared for Cleopatra. The king would never suspect that Berenike would sacrifice her loyal servant in a last desperate effort to save herself. Cleopatra began to have doubts herself – could she have misunderstood her sister's intentions?

"Pour me one glass. I'll deal with you later," said the king.

The ghost of a smile passed across Berenike's face, but it was enough for Cleopatra. She *was* right. Berenike wouldn't think twice about poisoning a maid. After all she had done the same to Tryphaena, her own sister.

As her father raised the goblet from the tray, Cleopatra got up off her knees and shouted, "Stop! Don't drink that!"

The hushed courtiers all turned in her direction.

"Have you no manners?" shouted a Roman. "Get out."

"No, Father! Stop! It's me, Princess Cleopatra."

A man next to her laughed in disbelief but the king put down the glass. He climbed off the platform and walked towards her.

"My daughter Cleopatra?" he murmured doubtfully. "But she's dead… Let me see you, girl."

Cleopatra looked up. She knew how much she had changed. Pshereni hadn't recognized her in Dendera and since then another year had passed. Suddenly she remembered the amulet Nechutes had returned and untied it from around her neck.

"I know I look different, but here's the amulet you gave me."

She held it out, frantically hoping that he would know her. He toyed with the charm, turning it over and over in the palm of his hand, and studying her intently.

"Your Majesty, Cleopatra died over two years ago," Berenike called. "This servant is an imposter."

The king ignored her. He looked like he'd seen a ghost. Then at last he said, "Where have you been?"

Cleopatra felt giddy with relief.

"With Iras. She kept me hidden in Upper Egypt. I came back as soon as I heard of your return."

"You are fearless," he said with pride. "I should have known you were too clever to be caught. Mark Antony," he said, turning to the tall man beside him, "you shall have the honour of being the first Roman to meet Princess Cleopatra."

Just then there was a retching sound. Lysandra was clutching her stomach. She was bent double, choking and spluttering.

"Help me," she gasped, staring imploringly at her mistress.

"I overheard Berenike and Pshereni making a plan. The wine was poisoned," said Cleopatra. "I was trying to warn you and now look what's happened."

Lysandra, who was twisting in pain, lost her balance and fell to the floor, crying out pitifully.

"Daughter, you did what you could," her father said

gently, patting her shoulder. Then he called out to two guards by the door, "You – take the maid away. See if anything can be done for her."

Lysandra was picked up and carried out. Her tongue was already swelling and she was struggling to breathe. *She hasn't got a chance*, thought Cleopatra.

The king turned back to the platform, shaking with anger, just in time to see Berenike dashing for the door.

"Grab her!" he shouted.

Two soldiers caught Berenike's arms. She kicked and scratched in a frantic effort to get away but they were too strong for her and she was dragged back to the king.

"Berenike and you, Pshereni, my own priest; Cleopatra has just proved you both traitors."

Pshereni was trembling uncontrollably. The colour had drained from Berenike's face and the soldiers that held her were supporting her weight.

"Father, please forgive me. I beg you to forgive me."

"I can't," the king answered. "You must both pay for your betrayal so that every man, woman and child in Egypt will know the price of treason. Every witness here will spread the news of your punishment throughout this kingdom."

"Sire, I beseech you," wailed Pshereni.

"Please, Father, I promise before Isis that I will never disobey you again," begged Berenike.

"I'm about to make certain of that," Ptolemy answered grimly. "Men, take Pshereni away and make him drink that wine he was so keen for me to have. Berenike, you must pay now."

"Father, no!"

"Gag her," said the king to the soldiers, "I will not hear another word from those deceitful lips."

A black scarf was tied tightly around Berenike's mouth. Her muffled screams were the only sound in the room.

"Now behead her," ordered the king. "She is no daughter of mine. Cleopatra alone has shown herself loyal and brave."

Cleopatra averted her eyes as the soldier pulled out a sword. Although she hated Berenike, she couldn't bear to watch and she flinched as she heard a swish and a gasp from the room. When she looked back, Berenike's severed head lay at the king's feet in a puddle of crimson blood while her body twitched on the polished floor.

"Princess, come up here," said the king from the platform. But Cleopatra's mind was already elsewhere.

"Father, I can't," she said. "There's someone who helped me. I need to see if he's still alive."

39

CLEOPATRA and Charmian retraced their steps as fast as they could to the room where they had left Nechutes. The king and his men hurried along behind them.

When they reached the door, Cleopatra put her ear to it. Nothing. Could Nefer still be prowling around in there?

"Open it," said the king. "What are you waiting for?"

"Berenike's leopard is tied up inside. We've got to be careful."

Her father turned to the Roman, Mark Antony.

"Are you ready for this?"

He nodded, pulled out a dagger, and then gently turned the door handle and looked into the room.

"There's no danger any more," he said.

Cleopatra rushed in to see Nefer lying on the floor with the chain still around her neck. Her amber eyes were lifeless and her great paws limp. The poison had worked, but where was Nechutes? There was no sign of him.

Her father and Mark Antony hurried over to examine Nefer.

"How was she killed?" said Ptolemy. "I can't see any wound."

On the marble floor, just beyond the body, Cleopatra spotted a fragment of the glass amphora, which must have shattered into a thousand pieces when it was dropped. Some of the deadly powder it contained was scattered around.

"Don't touch that stuff," she cried out. "It's the poison that killed Lysandra."

Her father jumped back.

"Get someone to clean it up immediately," he ordered a soldier who was standing by the door. "I suppose that's how your friend killed the animal."

"Where can Nechutes be?" said Cleopatra to Charmian. Terrible thoughts were going through her mind. Nefer couldn't have eaten the whole of him, could she? But how else could he have vanished?

Just then Charmian shrieked, "Look at this!"

She was pointing to a spot just beyond her feet. Cleopatra hurried over. The floor was tiled with crimson marble streaked with white but when she looked closely she could distinctly see blood.

"There's a trail," said Charmian.

Quickly both girls followed the spots of blood across the room to the linen curtain behind which they had hidden from Berenike. Cleopatra yanked it back.

Nechutes lay on the floor curled up like a baby. His legs and arms had gashes across them where Nefer had struck him and on his chest there was a deep cut. His tunic was stained red and blood was leaking onto the floor. Near his hand was a spilled jug of water. He must have crawled across the room to try to clean his wounds, but collapsed with the effort.

Cleopatra got down on her knees and rolled him onto his side. His arm flopped down limply.

"Nechutes. Nechutes," she said softly, shaking his shoulder. There was no response.

She shook him again.

"It's me, Mayum. Can you hear me?"

She searched his face for any flicker of life, but it was pale and blank.

"Daughter, you must prepare yourself for the worst," said her father gently.

"Oh no," said Cleopatra with her head in her hands. "I can't bear it. I came too late."

CLEOPATRA fell to her knees beside Nechutes. Tears blinded her. If only she had forbidden him to sacrifice himself. Charmian took her friend's hand.

"You had to leave him," she said. "You had no choice. Nechutes understood that. He was the bravest boy I ever knew."

"Come, Cleopatra," said her father, holding out a hand. "Leave him now. I will make sure the priests prepare him for the next life as if he were a prince. He'll want for nothing."

Cleopatra shook her head. She couldn't abandon Nechutes yet.

Gently she lifted his pale head onto her lap. Did she imagine it or, as she put him down, did he let out the tiniest of groans?

"Father," she said urgently. "I'm sure I heard him moan. I think he's alive."

"He can't be," said her father. "Look at his injuries. Nobody could survive them."

Mark Antony leant over and put his head to Nechutes's chest. He listened intently.

"By the gods, I think she's right." He looked up, his face full of wonder. "His heartbeat is faint but it's there."

"But look how he's bleeding," said the king. "Who can save him?"

"Diodorus," said Cleopatra quickly. "He'll be at the Museion. If anyone can help him he can."

Twenty minutes later Diodorus arrived carrying his leather bag. He hurried over to Nechutes, carefully rolled him onto his back, and examined him.

Cleopatra watched her tutor's every move.

"Can you do anything?" she asked at last, unable to contain herself any longer.

"He's still losing a lot of blood, I need to stop it," answered Diodorus.

He crushed some willow leaves, bark, honey and coriander into a sticky paste. "Princess, Charmian, I need your help. Hold him still while I dress his wounds. This will hurt him."

The girls each held down a leg and an arm. Nechutes winced as the paste was applied.

"Well, Diodorus, will he live?" asked the king when all the wounds had been treated.

"With care and good nursing, he should recover," said Diodorus. "But he will be weak for many months."

Cleopatra felt like cheering.

"Father, we can keep him here, can't we?"

"Of course," said the king. "He will receive the best care Alexandria has to give."

41

CLEOPATRA rose early. Her father was being re-crowned today and she would officially be declared his heir. When he heard the story of her escape from Alexandria and of her time in Bahri, Ptolemy had declared that there was no more fitting person to succeed him. Cleopatra had shown courage, bravery and loyalty, all the qualities that a queen would need.

For two months now she had been immersed in palace life again, going to the temple and meeting ambassadors and senior courtiers. Whenever she had a spare moment she visited Nechutes who was being nursed by Charmian in a room close to her apartment. As Diodorus had forecast he made slow but steady progress. Within a week he was sitting up in bed and within a month he was strong enough to walk around. The wounds were deep and he would be scarred but he would make a full recovery.

"I've never been so comfortable," he joked as he sat up in bed, wolfing down a plate of beef stew and Cleopatra was certain that he would soon be up and about, sailing on his beloved river.

Not long after her return, Cleopatra had asked for Iras to be collected from Bahri and brought back to the palace. After much scolding her nurse forgave her for disappearing so abruptly. Now only Apollodorus was still missing.

Iras and Charmian helped Cleopatra into the dress she was to wear for the coronation. The robe was made from pure, white linen so fine that it felt weightless. Around her shoulders she wore a collar six inches wide, encrusted with gold and coral. On each arm was a gold snake bracelet. Her hair was tucked away under a wig made up of hundreds of tiny plaits of human hair, stuck down with beeswax and interwoven with turquoise stones that clicked and clacked pleasantly as she moved her head.

Iras carefully painted round her eyes with black kohl and then rubbed some ochre on her cheeks to redden them.

"You truly look like a queen of Egypt," Charmian said when Iras had finished.

Cleopatra couldn't help feeling nervous. She was expected to speak to the crowd that afternoon and she didn't know what to say. She might look like a queen, but would she feel and sound like one?

The morning was taken up with prayers. After the service they headed off towards the amphitheatre. Priests led the way, followed by dancers and bands. Next came a regiment of soldiers, the royal children, and finally the king, in the double crown of Egypt.

As Ptolemy the Twelfth walked along, every hundred yards or so a man or woman ducked under the ropes that separated the parade from the crowds and fell at his feet, begging him to intervene in a dispute. As custom demanded, he stopped, listened and delivered his judgement. The third time, two women stopped the king. They must have had a complicated problem for the parade was delayed for many minutes while everybody waited in the midday sun. One wrung her hands and the other wailed. It seemed they would be here for some time.

Then the king beckoned for Cleopatra to join him.

"Daughter, these women are distraught. They are from Faiyum. This one," pointing at the shorter one, "says that her field is barren because the other one has diverted the canal."

"I have children who will starve next year if I cannot grow any food," sobbed the shorter woman.

"But this woman also has children," said the king wearily. "She says if we switch the canal back, her children will also go hungry as her field will then be dry. Who should we favour? I cannot choose."

The king was clearly frustrated but Cleopatra didn't want to condemn either family to starvation. There must be another way but she needed to know more.

She took the shorter woman's hand to try to calm her down.

"In previous years, were both fields good?"

"Yes."

"But this flood there has not been enough water for the two of you?"

"No," interjected the other. "So I took more, but I didn't realize what it would do to her."

"And you say you are from Faiyum. Are you close to the river?"

She had sailed through the area on the way back to Alexandria. It was a rich, fertile plain criss-crossed with canals as far as the eye could see.

"No," answered both women in unison. "We are several miles away."

Cleopatra remembered a lunch with Cheti when he had complained about corrupt priests. It must have something to do with the temple.

"Father," she said, "the flood has been good this year. Water is plentiful and yet it is not reaching these women. It must be that somewhere between these women's fields and the Nile, a canal has collapsed and that is why not enough water is reaching them. I would instruct the temple to get repairs done immediately, then both neighbours can be happy again and all the children can be fed."

Her father smiled.

"Good," he said and instructed a soldier to send the order.

He squeezed her hand.

"Every day I am reminded what a good choice I have

made in you as my heir. Now return to your place."

Cleopatra smiled nervously. She was pleased that her father had confidence in her but did she really have the wisdom required of a queen?

As she walked back to her place she looked around her. Just as when she had been to the festival in Dendera, there were people everywhere – on the roofs of the mud houses, at the windows and in the streets.

Suddenly a glint caught her eye. A medal attached to a man's tunic was shining in the sunlight. It was a golden fly, an honour given to only a small number of soldiers for exceptional bravery. She had only ever known one man who was entitled to wear it. She walked over to congratulate its owner and, as she did, her heart quickened. Could it be? In front of her, miraculously, stood her loyal guard.

"Apollodorus, you've come back," she said.

He smiled and pointed at the medal. "Just like that fly."

Cleopatra sighed. "I've been so worried. Where have you been?"

"Working along the desert trade routes," he answered, "as far away from Berenike as possible. When I was last in Asyut, I heard about the king's return and the coronation. I knew that if you were alive you'd be here, so I came straight back."

"I could easily have missed you in this crowd," exclaimed Cleopatra.

"Fate has always been looking out for you, Princess, of

that I am certain."

Cleopatra laughed. It certainly felt that way now.

The band was striking up again, signifying that the king was ready to move. "Apollodorus, I'm going to have to join the parade. Will you come to the palace tonight? I would like you to rejoin my service."

"I'd be honoured," replied her guard.

For the rest of the procession, Cleopatra was in a daze of happiness. Apollodorus was back. Iras was with her and now Charmian as well. Nechutes would be her eyes and ears in the countryside, Diodorus in the city. These were people that had proved their loyalty to her and that she could rely on in the difficult years that lay ahead. They would help her have the necessary wisdom.

As the king's children entered the stadium, the roar from the crowd was deafening. Cleopatra took her place on a stage made of solid silver. Moments later the king himself walked into the amphitheatre. After the prayers of the morning, it was time for him to demonstrate his fitness to be king. First he ran around a circuit of flags marked out in the shape of Egypt. Then he took a bow and four arrows, turned to the north, pulled the bow taut and shot the first arrow into the dust on the far side of the stadium. He then turned and shot again, east, and then south and then west. As each arrow hit the ground the spectators shouted their approval and a flock of birds were released into the blue sky.

"The king has run round the circumference of his

realm. He has shot down his enemies from all points on the compass," boomed a priest in Egyptian, "and now the birds will fly to every land to spread the news that Ptolemy the Twelfth is again King of Egypt. May he rule forever."

The crowd cheered.

The king raised his hands to speak.

"My people, one day I will have to leave Egypt and make my journey to the other world. Today, I wish to name my heir."

He waited a moment while his words of Greek were translated into Egyptian. Cleopatra gulped. Her heart pounded. What was he going to say?

"My daughter is a true child of Egypt. She was raised in Alexandria and educated by our greatest scholars at the Museion. She has worshipped at the temple of Isis and is well versed in our religion," continued the king. "She has travelled widely in our land and is blessed with a fluency in many languages. When I was forced to leave Egypt she was loyal and brave. I know that she has the spirit to lead our country to glory and I declare before you all that today I name Princess Cleopatra as my heir. Daughter, please come forward."

Cleopatra was overcome. She felt honoured and overawed. While the king's words were translated she had a few seconds to compose herself, then she climbed down off the stage and walked towards him. The king raised her hand in his, as if displaying her to his people.

"Say something to them, Child," he whispered.

Cleopatra's mind went blank. What was she to say to this expectant crowd? And then the words that Apollodorus had spoken came to her –"Fate is looking out for you" – and gave her confidence and a voice. She knew that this was what the gods wanted. With a wave of her hand she dismissed the translator and spoke clearly in Egyptian to her people.

"I swear before all of you and before Isis that I will serve this country faithfully and will try to look after your happiness and prosperity. Egypt can be a great land again, free and independent. I dedicate myself to this goal and to you, the country of my birth – Egypt."

And in her heart she knew that this was what fate wanted from her and she was determined to be true to her people and to her words.

THE END

WHAT HAPPENED NEXT

IN 51 BC, four years after his return from Rome, King Ptolemy the Twelfth died. Cleopatra was crowned queen at the age of just seventeen and despite her youth, she ruled wisely, concentrating on increasing the wealth of her people.

Two years later she faced a dilemma. The Roman General, Pompey, asked her for supplies to support his power struggle against Julius Caesar. Pompey was the conqueror of the Eastern Roman Empire; Julius Caesar had been successful in the West. Both now wanted to rule the whole Empire. Cleopatra felt obliged to support Pompey because he had helped restore her father to the Egyptian throne, but this was very unpopular with the people of Alexandria who wanted nothing more to do with Rome.

Prince Ptolemy, now aged thirteen and envious of his sister's power, took advantage of the situation, drove her into exile and then crowned himself King of Egypt.

Cleopatra was determined to regain the throne. She raised an army, which she intended to lead in battle against her disloyal younger brother, but changes in Rome overtook her. In 48 BC Julius Caesar defeated Pompey in a great battle and sailed into Alexandria.

Now the most powerful man in the world, he took charge of the royal palace and ordered Prince Ptolemy and Cleopatra to dismiss their armies and meet with him so that he could settle their dispute. Cleopatra realized that it was vital she get to Caesar first but there was no way for her to enter the city safely as it was surrounded by her brother's troops so she came up with an ingenious plan. She rowed across the harbour in a small boat and moored below the great palace walls. Here she was met by her faithful guard, Apollodorus. He wrapped her in an oriental rug tied with cord, slung her over his shoulder and casually entered the palace. Then he carried his precious bundle right into Caesar's private apartment, unrolled the carpet and Cleopatra tumbled out. Caesar was so enchanted with the bravery and charm of the twenty-one-year-old queen that he fell in love with her then and there.

Prince Ptolemy was furious when he saw Cleopatra and Caesar together the next day. He stormed out of the palace shouting that he had been betrayed and then laid siege to it. A decisive, bloody battle was fought in the harbour. Flames ravaged Prince Ptolemy's fleet and set light to a number of buildings at the water's edge, including the famous Museion. Thousands of irreplaceable scrolls, collected by more than nine generations of scholars and philosophers, were consumed by the fire.

Prince Ptolemy drowned in the Nile while trying to

escape the battlefield. Caesar stayed in Egypt for a further three months before moving on to fight other wars for the Roman Empire. He was so impressed with the young queen that Rome did not annex the country but left Cleopatra as ruler and she continued her work to rebuild her country.

Five years later, on the Ides of March 44 BC, Julius Caesar was stabbed to death by a group of Roman senators, envious of his power. General Mark Antony was one of the potential heirs to Caesar. This was the same Mark Antony that Cleopatra had met as a child in Alexandria when her father returned from Rome. Caesar's nephew, Octavian, was also claiming Caesar's inheritance and so began another feud over who should lead the Roman Empire. This quarrel resulted in a splitting of the Empire with Mark Antony controlling the East and Octavian the West.

During this difficult time Cleopatra's goal was always to keep Egypt independent. She realized that with Julius Caesar gone, Egypt was again vulnerable to being taken over. In order to stop this she needed an ally and she chose Mark Antony.

To win him over she sailed to him in a golden barge with purple sails and silver oars. The boat was rowed by her maids who were dressed as mermaids while Cleopatra was dressed as Venus, the goddess of love. Mark Antony was bewitched. They returned together to Alexandria.

For four years Cleopatra and Mark Antony were allies and lovers. He allowed her to continue to rule Egypt, and in return she provided him with support in his struggle against Octavian. Mark Antony won a number of territories in battle, which he gave to Cleopatra.

During this period Cleopatra almost succeeded where many kings and queens before her had failed. Despite inheriting a country crippled by chronic misrule and debt, through intelligence, persuasion and cunning she turned the situation around to such an extent that Egypt's empire was expanding rather than shrinking.

But between 36 BC and 31 BC Octavian built up his troops and his support in Rome. In 31 BC Octavian and Mark Antony had a decisive last battle and Mark Antony was badly defeated.

In 30 BC Octavian reached the shores of Alexandria. Mark Antony and Cleopatra were trapped in the city, surrounded by Roman troops. In desperation Mark Antony stabbed himself in the stomach, rather than be captured by Octavian. As he lay bleeding to death from his wounds, friends carried him to Cleopatra who was hiding from the approaching Romans and he died in her arms.

When Octavian arrived, he took Cleopatra prisoner. He planned to take her to Rome where she would be led through the town in chains, but Cleopatra had no intention of being humiliated. She arranged for a basket of figs to be brought to her in which was hidden a tiny asp, a poisonous snake. Bravely, Cleopatra took the serpent and held it against her body until it bit her.

Several hours later on August 12th 30 BC, the last queen of Egypt was found dead on a golden couch. She was thirty-nine years old. On her arm were two pricks left by the snake's fangs. In ancient Egypt it was believed that death by snake bite secured immortality.

Both of her maids, Charmian and Iras, who had served her loyally throughout her life, chose to die with their queen, probably by taking poison. When the soldiers entered the room Iras lay dying at Cleopatra's feet while Charmian, scarcely able to stand, was tottering at her bedside, trying to adjust the queen's crown.

"This is a fine deed, Charmian," one of the Romans shouted angrily.

"Yes," she replied, "it is a fine deed, and fitting for a princess descended from so many kings."

These were her last words before she too died like her mistress and Iras.

On her death Cleopatra passed into legend. She was remembered as a brave and beautiful queen who bewitched both Julius Caesar and Mark Antony, but she was also an able monarch who ruled Egypt justly in difficult times.

Throughout her life she tried to keep her country free from Roman domination, cleverly playing off one Roman against another. After her death Egypt became a

Roman province, ending a three-thousand-year-old civilization, and it was ruled by Rome until that Empire fell apart five hundred years later.

Author's Notes

WHEN I first began to research the early years of Cleopatra's life I was surprised by how little historians know. It is not certain who her mother was or which of her brothers and sisters were full blood siblings. And there is little evidence about where she spent the two years while her father went to Rome.

When Cleopatra was a child, Egypt was a poorly governed country struggling to come to terms with the rise of the Roman Empire. I have tried to be historically accurate about the politics of the time and the key characters. Ptolemy the Twelfth, Pshereni, Apollodorus, Diodorus, Berenike, Tryphaena, Arsinoe and the princes are all real people, but, of course, in most instances I have had to imagine their personalities. We do have some clues from the past. Ptolemy was known as the "Flute Player" and for his over-indulgence in wine. Berenike was certainly ambitious. She took advantage of her father's escape to Rome to seize power, and was beheaded on his return. Iras and Charmian did remain loyal to their mistress to the end, although we know little about their origins and how they came to serve the queen. Finally, Cleopatra must have been a clever child as she became a famous linguist and scholar. She must also have been daring and resourceful. Not only did she survive a tumultuous period when her father was in Rome, she emerged as his chosen heir.

Notes From the Past

THE NILE: At almost 7,000 km, the River Nile is the world's longest river. Its annual flood, caused by rainfall in the Ethiopian mountains, was crucial to Ancient Egypt. It replenished the soil with rich silts. Water was also captured in pools to irrigate the land during the rest of the year. This pattern of agriculture did not change in Egypt until the completion of the Aswan Dam in the 1960s.

BOATS: Travel by river was much easier than by road and so the Nile became Egypt's main highway. Boats rowed with the current when heading north and were blown by the prevailing winds when heading south. Every town had a quay and the wealthy often had their own private harbours. Magnificent barges were even built for the gods and goddesses.

TEMPLES: During the time of Cleopatra, high stone walls surrounded the temples. The inside was considered sacred and ordinary people were not permitted to enter. Priests went into the temples through a pylon – two sloping towers with a large central doorway. These were decorated with carvings, hieroglyphs and good luck charms.

THE GODDESS ISIS: The Ancient Egyptians worshipped many gods. By the time of Cleopatra, Isis had become the most popular. Egyptians thought of her as the perfect wife and mother. She was also believed to be responsible for the annual flood of the Nile. Isis was usually portrayed with a sun disc over her head.

AMULETS: Amulets have been found by archaeologists all over Egypt. People wore them for luck and to ward off danger. As soon as a baby was born an amulet would be tied around its wrist.

Scarabs, a type of beetle, were the most common form. The poor wore scarabs carved from stone. Only the very wealthy could afford gold.

THE GOLDEN FLY: The very bravest soldiers were awarded the golden fly in Ancient Egypt. It was equivalent to a military medal. The fly was chosen as a symbol of dedication and persistence because however often a fly is swatted away, it always returns.

SCHOOLS: Ancient Egyptians valued education highly but it was only for boys. Girls were expected to stay at home with their mothers. If a boy learnt to read and write he could get a well-paid job as a scribe. Parents tried hard to send their sons to school but it was expensive and most could not afford it.

WRITING: Ancient Egyptians began writing over 5,000 years ago using a script called hieroglyphs. This is one of the oldest written languages. Hieroglyphs are unusual as some of them stand for sounds and some for objects. The twenty-four signs representing sounds might be the foundation of the alphabet we use today.

The rough paper used in Ancient Egypt was made from the stem of the papyrus plant. Papyrus grew along the banks of the Nile. To make a sheet of papyrus, thin strips of the stem were arranged in layers, one horizontally and the other vertically, and then squashed under stones. Pens were made from reeds and ink from crushed minerals.

Most Ancient Egyptians were illiterate and could not read the hieroglyphs carved on pylons and statues.

SNAKES: There are many species of poisonous snake in Egypt, such as the cobra, viper and asp. To protect themselves from snakes, Ancient Egyptians wore amulets, made offerings to the gods and slept with garlic cloves.

THE YEAR: The Ancient Egyptians were the first people to develop a calendar that kept time with the sun and the seasons. They did this by dividing the year into three periods – Akhet, when the Nile flooded, Peret, the sowing season, and Shemu, the harvest. Each season was made up of four months of thirty days. This gave a year of 360 days so five festival days were added. The Romans adapted the Egyptian scheme by adding leap years. This forms the basis of our own modern calendar.

TIME: The Ancient Egyptians invented the twenty-four hour clock. Priests divided the night into twelve hours using the rotation of the stars. The day was also divided into twelve hours. Hours varied in length throughout the year. In winter a daytime hour would be shorter than a night-time hour as the sun rose later and set earlier. Egyptians used sundials and water clocks to measure time.

MEDICINES: Ancient Egyptian doctors were famed for their skills. Doctors studied in temples and at the Museion in Alexandria. Egyptian doctors had to make their own medicines from plants, oils, herbs and minerals. They also used magic spells and amulets on their patients.

BOUDICA

THE SECRETS OF THE DRUIDS

Read an extract from
the second book in the thrilling
BEFORE THEY WERE FAMOUS series.

Available now!

SPRING, AD 43

"HOW long to go now?"

"Boudica, I told you not to ask me again," said a stout woman, stirring a pot of stew. An older woman was stripping meat from a bone. All three were huddled close to a fire, their cheeks glowing in the heat.

"Please, Hendra. Just tell me when you think they'll come?"

The heavy woman put down her spoon.

"Let me see. Last night they'll have camped at Bodras. We're a good day's ride away, so I reckon the earliest you can expect them is when the sun touches the tip of the forest. That's if they make good time. What do you think, Argent?"

"Sounds about right to me."

The girl jumped up, ran to the far side of the wattle house, and pulled back a fur covering a doorway. A blast of icy air sent smoke from the fire whirling. Boudica looked across the valley to the wood, her red hair billowing in the bitterly cold draught.

"That's not long; I need to go."

She stepped out into the misty afternoon light.

"Boudica, come back. You've got to help. There's a feast to get ready."

The girl reappeared.

"I will. I've just got to get something for my father. It's his present. It must be ready when he comes."

"You haven't even got a fur on. You'll freeze," called Hendra, but there was no response.

"She's wild, that one," complained Argent, pushing a strand of grey hair out of her eyes. Her gnarled fingers glistened with fat from the meat. "I won't be sorry when she leaves the tribe. You never know what she's up to."

"She's wild all right," said Hendra, "but I'll miss her. She's the bravest girl I've ever known. You've seen the way she rides a horse: none of the boys can touch her. Anyway she hasn't seen her family for over a year. You can't blame her for being excited."

The door creaked open and a tall woman with frizzy, black hair entered. She was wearing a blue tartan dress pinned with a brooch and a thick torc, a heavy band of twisted gold, round her neck.

Hendra nudged Argent and said under her breath, "Watch out, Queen Cartimandua's here."

Both women hastily got to their feet.

"Where's Boudica?" demanded the queen.

"She's gone out, ma'am. I'm sure she'll be back soon."

Queen Cartimandua pursed her lips.

"Hendra, that girl is supposed to be in your care, but you never seem to know where she is."

"Sorry, ma'am."

"I want to see her. She must look respectable when her parents turn up, otherwise they'll wonder what we've been doing with her. Do you understand?"

"Yes, ma'am. I'll go and find her straightaway."

Hendra had a shrewd idea that Boudica would be with Culann, the town blacksmith. The two were as thick as thieves. She tried to picture Boudica when she'd left. As usual her hair was tangled, there was almost certainly mud on her skirt and her hem was bound to be ripped. Somehow it always was. And that was before she went to Culann's. She'd be even grubbier when she got back. Hendra sighed. It was impossible to keep Boudica from looking scruffy.

Boudica felt like jumping for joy as she ran through the town. She was going to be reunited with her family. She hadn't seen them since last spring when she'd left her tribe, the Iceni, to journey northwards. Aged eleven, the children of the royal household and of the king's most senior warriors were expected to spend a year with another tribe. Jodoc, Boudica's father, was principal counsellor to Antedios, King of the Iceni, and so Boudica had been sent away to the Brigantes. Relations between this tribe and the Iceni had been difficult ever since Queen Cartimandua inherited the Brigantian throne. The Iceni hoped an exchange would improve things. Now Boudica had done her bit and would soon be heading home.

She arrived at a wattle building. It was smaller than the other houses in Canna, the largest Brigantian town, and was set apart. Despite the perishing wind, the door was open. A wiry hunting dog trotted out and barked half-heartedly.

"Mutta, don't be silly, it's me," said Boudica, patting the dog's head. "Those puppies are making you such a worrier."

She gave the dog a reassuring stroke and went inside, where the singeing heat of a furnace dominated a room crowded with a jumble of dusty mallets, ingots, and piles of charcoal. In the far corner was a wicker basket with three tiny puppies in it. They were so young they looked like grey balls of fur. Mutta settled down to feed her litter.

A lanky boy of thirteen stood next to the hearth, delicately knocking a ball of clay with a hammer. The boy's hair was streaked with soot but that did little to diminish its amazing colour – a vivid ginger, not auburn or red-tinged, but bright orange, like a piece of rusted iron. On top of gangly legs and arms that had yet to fill out, this wiry, luminescent mop announced to even the most casual of observers that the boy was not from these parts. The Brigantes were dark, bronzed, and stocky, everything that Culann was not. Boudica had noticed him as soon as she arrived in Canna and had decided then and there that they would be friends. After all, the two flame-haired children could have been brother and sister. It had taken persistence, as Culann was a natural loner, but her determination had paid off. He was the only person in the town she would miss.

"Hello," called Boudica.

Culann turned round, his smutty, freckled face full of concentration. "Stay there," he ordered.

Despite this instruction, Boudica tiptoed over. She watched quietly as Culann tapped the terracotta sphere, skilfully chipping away chunks of clay. A sliver of bronze appeared. It grew and grew, and a tiny dagger, adorned with fine red and blue lines that twisted like the wind, emerged before her eyes.

"It's lovely!" Boudica couldn't help exclaiming. "It's just what I wanted."

Culann turned round, exasperated.

"I thought I told you to stand back," he said, pushing an unruly curl out of his eye.

"I'm sorry. Have I ruined the surprise?"

Culann rolled his eyes and smiled.

"I suppose not, as it's not really for you."

He handed her the miniature dagger and she examined it carefully. It looked like a toy, but the glinting blade was sharp. The metal handle was carved with the swirling lines that she had come to associate so strongly with the Brigantes. It was traditional for a returning child to give a gift to their father, and this would be perfect.

"Culann, thank you so much. My father will love it,"

she said at last.

Just then a horse thundered past, its rider shouting, "They're coming into the valley. The Iceni are here."

Boudica looked across at the wood. The sun was still way above the tips of the trees. Her parents had made much better time than Hendra had forecast. Suddenly she was gripped with excitement.

"I've got to go. I'll see you at the feast tonight."

"Where are you off to in such a hurry?"

"I'm going to meet my parents and ride with them into the town."

"Boudica, don't. The queen won't want you to and you're covered in soot," Culann called after her but she was gone.

Moments later Hendra came in, panting.

"Where's Boudica?" she asked. "I thought she'd be with you."

"She was. You just missed her. She's gone to meet the Iceni."

"Oh no." Hendra looked horrified. "Couldn't you stop her?"

Culann smiled. "What do you think?"

"Well, I only hope the prince who's replacing her will be less trouble," said Hendra, shaking her head. "He can't be any more."